SCEPTER OF SOREN

by Robert Michael Taylor Sr.

Copyright © 2023 Robert Michael Taylor Sr.

All rights reserved.

ISBN-13:979-8-9882828-1-5

Table of Contents

A stranger in the Forest
1

The Runes in the Dirt and the Smoke in the Hearth
7

Perils and Wonders of the Strange Land
9

The Cloud and the Scepter
19

The Seer's Warning
27

The Kingdom of Elves: A Divided Realm
34

The Elf Alliance
37

The March of the Goblins
40

The Swamp Ambush
43

The Truce of the Dark Elves
49

Arrival at the Palace
53

The Goblin Proposal
62

Plains of Peril
70

The Battle of the Bluff
81

The Battle on the Plains of Leon.

The Chosen One and the Staff of Power — 88
A Prophecy Fulfilled — 93
The Power of the Scepter — 98
The Battle of the Walls: A Last Stand for the Elvish Kingdom — 104
Breaking the Spell — 109
Waking in Darkness — 117
Trapped in the Cavern of the Tiny Warriors — 123
The Demon's Flight — 125
A Demon in the Cabin — 133
The Ferryman — 135
Hope and Courage — 144
The Fall of the Dark One — 146
154

CHAPTER ONE

A stranger in the Forest

The young man traveled the forest path as fast as the deer that had resided there before something had laid its cold hand upon this, his forest, the forest of his ancestors. Hearing a loud crashing noise, he stopped, holding his breath. Slowly swiveling his head in all directions, he waited, straining his ears, but when no other sounds ensued, he shrugged his shoulders, deciding it had been a dead branch toppling from one of the numerous tall trees.

Relaxing his stance, he wiped the sweat off his face with the back of his hand. He looked down and saw part of the leather strip binding his leggings gone. Letting a sigh escape, he reached up and untied the strip of leather holding his shoulder-length blonde hair.

He turned, surveying the forest with gray, almost translucent eyes before bending down to repair his leggings, listening for any strange sounds that might come from the surrounding forest.

Finished, he stood up, inhaling the crisp morning air, enjoying the familiar smell. Looking around once more with the practiced eye of a hunter, he turned, disappearing into the dense foliage, leaving nothing behind to show he had passed this way. He traveled many more miles, the dead vegetation muffling his footfalls before he stopped to rest. He felt his ears pricked at the sound of running water. His throat was dry and parched; the water skin he carried long ago emptied. Pushing his way through the thick undergrowth, he walked into a small clearing. Seeing the gurgling spring, he unconsciously licked his dry lips in anticipation. Cautiously he made his way to its bank. Laying the bow and quiver of arrows that he carried down, he stared at the forest around him. Seeing nothing, he reached into his belt pouch and withdrew a small skinning knife. This he drove into the ground, his hand resting lightly on its leather hilt. Satisfied nothing lurked in the trees, he lay on his stomach noisily slurping the clear cool water. His thirst slackened, he rose to his knees, facing the sun and enjoyed the feel of the warmth on his face.

    If weariness had not beset him, he would have noticed the strange apparition that seemed to materialize from the trees on the far side of the clearing. A twig snapping caused the youth to jerk upright, bringing his knife with him. Clenching his left hand, he wondered what chance he would have at retrieving the bow that still lay on the ground, cursing himself for his mistake while staring across the space that separated him from the stranger leaning against one of the trees on the far side of the clearing. The sun shining in his face blinded him, causing him to mistake the figure for a hunter such as himself. Adjusting his eyes to the sun's brightness, his knees grew weak at the sight of the stranger before him. With a measured eye, he judged him to be a foot taller than his own six-foot frame as he felt clamminess come over him. The young man's eyes grew wider at seeing cloven hooves where the feet should have been as he also took in the coarse brown fur which extended from the creature's waist to the bottom of the hooves. A fiend, thought the youth, reaching for the bow that still lay on the ground, hoping to go unnoticed by the figure. Still leaning against the tree with an unconcerned look showing on his all-too-human face, he folded his massive arms across the immensity of his chest.

    The creature looked at the young man with amusement crinkling the corners of his dark green eyes that set above a wide flaring nose. Taking a deep breath and expelling it slowly, he casually reached up, scratching the long brown hair running to the middle of his back, then raked the antlers that stemmed from his head across the tree's bark, leaving deep furrows. Time stood still for the young man, standing transfixed at the sight.

    "What have we here?" spoke the strange being in a deep but musical voice.

    Startled out of his trance, the youth forgot the bow as he faced the creature, who now had a smile on his full lips. Seeing the smile, the youth recaptured his boldness that had slipped away at seeing the horned being so suddenly before him. He studied the face and saw it was as human as his own.

"Are you not afraid of being caught in the forest this night?"

"There is no reason to be feared," said the youth, finding his voice and unconsciously taking a step backward.

The manbeast stepped from the shade of the trees, and the young man noticed his upper body was covered in a fine, light brown down that ended at his neck.

"Why do you come here, child of the forest?" asked the strange apparition while stamping his hooves on the short grass of the clearing.

The youth could feel his heart beating rapidly and his pulse racing. "I come in search for what evil has befallen my village." Not taking his eyes from the visage before him, he wiped his sweating palms on the side of his leather breeches, wondering if this was the evil he sought.

"Brave words from one so young." The manbeast noticed the youth's anxiety and the terror building in his eyes. "It would be better for you to be home mayhap helping your mother."

The young man's anger rose at this remark, dispelling his terror. He stealthily reached again for the bow lying at his feet.

Noticing this, the horned being took another step toward the youth. "It would be wise for your hand not to touch that bow."

The young man's hand froze as if it was encased in ice.

"Are you not afraid of the dark witches of this forest? They would make a fine meal of you."

The young man's voice croaked, "The witches of the forest are but old wives' tales to be told around the campfire."

Stepping to within a few feet of the young man, the strange being cocked his head and said, "Are you so sure of this, my fearless young friend? My name is Loekor, of the horned ones. Who may you be?"

With Loekor towering above him, it caused the young man's legs to turn to rubber. It was hard for him not to turn and run, but pride would not let him do this. "I am Therseus, a hunter of the Keelon tribe." As he said this, he could feel his boldness slip away again to be replaced by fear at being so close to this oddity.

Seeing the youth's anxiety, he relaxed his stance and said, "You have no need to fear me, my young friend." Loekor knelt to quench his thirst from the clear, cold water dancing over the small rocks.

Thirst satisfied, he turned a critical eye toward the youth. "It is no jest when I say there are many dangers in the forest now."

"I fear not these dangers you speak of." He took measure of the strange being before him.

Loekor raised his head, scenting the air. "Well, my young Therseus, gather your bow and come share my camp. I fear darkness will soon approach us, and as I can see, you have yet to make camp."

Loekor turned his broad back. The sun slowly sinking, casting its last rays down into the clearing, he disappeared back into the forest with his voice drifting over his shoulder. "Come young Therseus, before night falls."

Therseus stooped to gather his bow and quiver of arrows. Impressed by the creature's boldness, he watched the creature's back as it vanished among the trees. He stood undecided, still not quite able to believe what he had seen. Finally, he followed out of curiosity. He, too, disappeared into the trees. Catching sight of his quarry through the last glimmer of light, he labored to catch up. A slight breeze rustled the boughs overhead, causing leaves to gently float to the ground in a slow dance as the young man ran past unheeded.

After a mile or so, they broke out into another clearing, this one much smaller than the one where they had their previous encounter. Therseus looked around appreciably at the small camp. It would be hard to attack from all but one side, the side they had just entered.

The smell of smoke wafted past his nose as Loekor rekindled a fire that had all but extinguished itself from lack of more fuel. Pangs of hunger stabbed at Therseus since he had not eaten that day. And seeing the bird roasting over the small flames intensified his hunger.

Loekor saw the young man unconsciously licking his lips while his eyes rested attentively on the golden brown bird and invited him to sit by the fire, passing a flask of wine to him.

"Will you not share this fowl with me?" Loekor asked, reaching for the bird and tearing away a leg, offering it to his young guest.

They sat quietly, eating and appraising each other as darkness fell, the fire illuminating the small camp.

Having finished his food, Loekor sipped the wine he had

retrieved from the young man. "I fear this fine wine has dulled my senses, but what better way to end a feast!" He lay back, propping his head upon his arms and gazing at the stars while waiting for Therseus to finish eating.

Therseus puzzled over his strange host while he ate. Where could such a being have come from?

Finished with his meal, Therseus could stand it no longer. "Would it offend you if I asked what sort of strange manbeast you are, and from whence you come?"

Loekor rolled over onto his stomach to better observe the young man. He wrinkled his brow in thought. After several moments, he threw back his head, and a hearty laugh escaped him. "I could ask you the same, Therseus."

A look of consternation passed over the young man's face before he, too, found the humor in this remark.

As the tension broke between the two, Loekor asked, "What of this evil you are intent upon avenging yourself on?" He could see the young man's face grow hard in the firelight, and a strong determination settle into his eyes.

"I know not what manner of evil it is, but I am sure it must be a great evil from the way the animals have fled the forest of my homeland." He grew silent as he stared into the fire.

"And what do the people of your village think of this menace you call evil?"

"There are no people." Therseus felt a catch in his throat. "I returned one day from hunting to find the village deserted." He continued to gaze into the fire, deep in his thought. A few minutes passed before he spoke again. "This is the reason I find myself traveling in this part of the forest. I seek the reason for my people's disappearance. I must find them, and if I can, release them from the evil that surely has borne them away. What brings you here, Loekor?" he asked while turning from the fire to gaze at the prone form lying on the ground.

"I, too, search for this evil that you speak of."

"How do you know of this evil?" asked the young man, a look of cunning crept upon his face causing his eyes to narrow. He crossed his arms across his chest and slumped forward, waiting for Loekor to relate his story.

Loekor rolled over onto his side, propping his head upon his arm to better see his young guest. "Two summers past a great seer and prophet of my tribe predicted this evil that you speak of, young friend. But before he could say what or where this evil was to be found, he fell over and was carried off by the wings of death. With his demise, I started my journey. Often, I have thought I acted foolishly in my haste to find this evil, or whatever it is. Several times I have started back to the forest of my homeland, only to have a feeling of unquiet settle over me and a nagging in my head that tells me to keep going until I find my answer." Loekor settled back, watching the small sparks from the fire climb into the air and disappear.

A thoughtful expression came to the young man as he regarded the figure before him. Both figures were silent, each wrapped up in their own thoughts as they enjoyed the heat radiating from the small fire. A damp chill had entered the air, with tendrils of mist slowly creeping along the ground and rising to envelop the trees in its damp embrace. It was quiet, with not even the sounds of insects to interrupt the tranquility that had settled over the forest. "This is strange," thought Theseus as drowsiness overtook him, and the sound of the crackling fire came to him in a distant sort of way, as if from a far distance.

Seeing the youth asleep, Loekor reflected back on the day he left his small village in Pandaria. He thought about how the youth sharing his camp had started out much as he had, even though their reasons were different. He understood what had prompted the youth, as even now, he could feel his heart tugging at him, beckoning him home. He visualized what it would be like to return home and find everything he held dear gone, as if it had been a dream in the first place. But was he not carrying his homeland in his heart? He would invite the youth to go with him. Were not their quests the same? He wanted to protect his village from an elusive evil that evaded him, and the young man wanted to restore his village as it had been, populated with the ones he held dear. With these thoughts, he slept as the last embers of the small fire lost their sparks of life.

CHAPTER TWO

The Runes in the Dirt and the Smoke in the Hearth

The forest buzzed with life, the whispers of leaves in the wind and the soft padding of animals on the damp forest floor. Far away, the mournful howl of a wolf echoed through the trees, a shiver-inducing sound to any who heard it. But deep within the heart of the forest, a small clearing exuded a peculiar stillness.

A diminutive figure occupied the center of the clearing, her hands weaving intricate patterns as she etched runes into the dirt with a gnarled stick. Her voice, barely audible, melded with the rustling leaves as she muttered her incantations. As she labored, a soft bluish light emanated from a nearby tree, casting an eerie, otherworldly glow upon the clearing. The woman appeared unfazed, lost in her own world as she continued her work.

Finally satisfied, she turned and ambled back, her youthful stride belying the age etched on her face. She entered a door camouflaged within the tree, which sealed itself silently behind her, leaving the bark unblemished. Inside, the old woman navigated the dimly-lit room and, after a thorough search, produced a small gilded chest.

With the chest in hand, she crossed the room to a modest stone hearth, the cold embers waiting to be stirred. She added fuel to the hearth, and small flames licked the blackened surface with a gentle crackling. Opening the chest, she scooped a handful of sparkling gold-colored powder and tossed it into the fire. Then, she perched on a stool, waiting patiently for the vision she knew would come.

As the powder sizzled, a dark violet cloud of smoke emerged, contained within the hearth, growing dense and nearly solid. She peered into the hypnotic fumes, anxiety building as she saw nothing but darkness. Leaning in, her nose nearly grazing the smoke, she sighed with relief as she discerned two figures lying on the ground in a deep slumber.

As she stared intently, the larger figure stirred and sat up, scanning the darkness with wariness in their eyes. It was then that she noticed the majestic antlers crowning the being's head. "Yes, you are the one," she thought to herself, her brow furrowing even deeper in concentration. With a graceful wave of her hand, the purplish cloud disintegrated, leaving a lingering, pungent scent in the air. The vision faded, and she leaned back on the small stool, allowing her thoughts to drift.

Her memories carried her away to other times, to long-forgotten days when the world was young and untamed, and she had fought alongside others in the brutal Goblin Wars. Immersed in these recollections, she relived the strife and struggle that had defined that era. With a heavy sigh, she remembered the centuries of bloodshed that had been necessary to end the war, a conflict that had nearly obliterated the world and scattered countless forgotten races to the winds.

Her shoulders slumped as she pondered the wizards and witches who, following the war, had exiled themselves from the realm of humankind, proclaiming that the era of magic was over. "Where are you now, my brave allies?" she mused, her worry etching deep lines on her face as she rocked back and forth on the small stool.

CHAPTER THREE

Perils and Wonders of the Strange Land

The young man awoke to the smell of cooking, and rolling over; he saw a small blackened pot hanging over a fire. He turned over, stretched, and looked toward a small bush close by, seeing a spider web with morning dew drops still hanging onto the threads, making it look like a many jeweled necklace. He felt goosebumps rise on his bare arms, as they made contact with the damp ground. Smiling, he laid his head back down and closed his eyes, only to jerk up, remembering where he was, and of his meeting with the strange being yesterday. It wasn't a dream, he mused, as he spied Loekor coming into the camp with what appeared to be a water flask slung across his shoulder.

"I see you are awake, my young friend," Loekor said in a musical voice, the notes being carried away on the morning breeze. "I was starting to wonder if you would wake this day," saying this, he walked over to the fire and sat the flask down. He held his hands over the fire and briskly rubbed them together. "There is a chill in the air this morning." He looked at the young man, smiling, as he saw his eyes grow wide. "Are you not used to my appearance? Come, come sit by the fire and warm yourself."

The young man eyed Loekor as he covered the short distance. "I am sorry. I did not mean to stare, but I do find you an oddity." Squatting, he, too, warmed his hands, still not able to take his eyes away from the stranger sitting with legs crossed on the other side of the fire, returning his look as a smile still played across his face. "I take no offense, my young friend, for I, too, had to get used to your appearance. It must be hard to walk on feet that resemble a duck's."

Hearing this, Therseus laughed with Loekor. Their laughter startled a lone squirrel that had been watching them among the branches. Therseus was pleased to see not all of the animals in the forest had disappeared.

A lone vulture circled far overhead, disappointed at the young man not being dead as it had first thought, seeing him lying on the ground. With a squawk, it soared across the red-tinted sky, soon only a dot as it searched further for its breakfast.

"Here," said Loekor, handing Therseus a wooden bowl he had retrieved from the pack resting by his side. "I think you will find this broth very rejuvenating." He searched the pack and produced another bowl, which he filled with the steaming fluid. The two ate in silence, with only the breeze echoing through the trees to break the quietness surrounding them.

Loekor thoughtfully stared over the rim of his bowl, wondering if he should tell Therseus of the strange vision that haunted his dreams, and drove his on, how it manifested itself, emanating from a dark mist within his mind to beckon him. He reminisced over this, visualizing it as he had seen it in so many of his dreams. How a fine mist would settle down in front of him while he sat unable to move his limbs. How the small figure would raise one hand and beckon him while it mouthed the word, "Come," in a silent plea. How the small figure would turn and let a mist swallow her up, and then it would rise and evaporate before him, only to leave him in darkness. He recalled it clear, as the young man before him tilted his bowl and finished the strong broth.

The young man rose, stretching his cramped limbs. He started to say something but refrained from this as he walked over to the place he had slept to retrieve his bow and quiver of arrows. He started off into the tall trees and wondered how best to ask, what he considered a new friend, or at least an ally, if he might join him. He was tired of the solitude of traveling alone, besides, he found solace in his company.

Loekor, seeing the strife which was plain on the young man's face, said, "I know we have just met, but it seems our quest bound us together. It would be foolish not to join forces. Is this not so?"

The young man spun around, relief and happiness showing on his face. "How did you know what was troubling me, Loekor?"

"It was written on your face. Mayhaps we'll be able to help one another on this journey. We should begin soon," he said while kicking dirt over the live coals, extinguishing the fire. "I must tell you though, I feel reluctant to leave this place. I find tranquility here in this small clearing." He paused at what he was doing and looked to Therseus. "Mayhap you should think on this, Therseus. It is a dangerous path I travel with many pitfalls, I'm sure."

"Where do we travel from here?" asked Therseus in answer. He walked over to where Loekor had his pack. Reaching down, he was surprised at finding he could lift it but a foot off the ground. He had always thought of himself as a stout lad.

Seeing this display caused merriment to crinkle the corners of his eyes, but Loekor held the chuckle that threatened to escape his lips. He turned, surveying the land before him lest Therseus see him. He did not want to embarrass the young man. "We travel to the Blue Forest of Lorn. We search for the witch that lives there, so legend says."

Therseus, thinking, could not recall a forest by that name. He had never traveled beyond the great forest of his homeland and doubted if anyone in his small village had, having been content with their forest and using it as their boundaries.

The red sun shone down on the two travelers, quickly dissipating the chill that had been in the air. Therseus could already feel the beads of sweat on his forehead as his body perspired in the early morning sun. He would be glad to re-enter the dark coolness of the surrounding forest. Out of the corner of his eye, he saw Loekor pick the pack up off the ground and sling it over his massive shoulders as easily as it was for him to carry his quiver of arrows.

"Would you mind carrying the water flask as this pack is heavy?" He gave Therseus a questioning glance. "The added weight of the flask would surely be too much for me," he said, hoping this would repair the young man's damaged ego.

Therseus slung the two flasks over his shoulder, not missing the fact that Loekor could carry them also as easily as he carried the pack, which did not seem to strain him at all. He marveled over Loekor's strength, glad he wasn't an enemy. He would be more than just a formidable foe.

Loekor set a brisk pace as they entered the forest, with the trees standing as silent sentinels. They traveled all day and finally walked out to find a broad plain before them. The sun turned the plains into a burnished orange as it sank slowly on the horizon. They decided to make camp there and cross the plains when the new day found them. As the dusky twilight chased away the darkness, the two travelers were well on their way.

They spied strange, elephantine animals grazing on the short grass of the rolling plains and tried to keep their distance, not knowing what the animals would do upon their intrusion. They did pass close enough to discern the animals had tusks, which they used to uproot small tufts of grass. The two travelers noticed the grass had abnormally long roots, and it was these the animals feasted on. One of the beasts raised its head and trumpeted through a short nose as it noticed the small audience watching them. It glared at them balefully through orange eyes, easily as big as a handspan, raising the long coarse hair on its back like a porcupine when disturbed. It also raised a clawed foot, intent on charging the two small pests, but on seeing this, the two travelers quickly hurried away while glancing over their shoulders to make sure the beast was not following.

Therseus had to pick up his pace to keep up with Loekor, who seemed never to tire. Though he sweated heavily and drank a lot of water, he perceived the opposite with his friend, who didn't seem to perspire and refused water when Therseus asked him if he was not thirsty. After half a day's travel, Loekor called a stop so that his young friend might rest, after noticing the strain the fast travel was causing him.

As they sat resting under the relentless red sun, Therseus asked, "What sort of strange beasts were those we passed?"

Loekor leaned heavily against the pack and looked out into the distance that was far beyond the sight of Therseus. Raising his head and scenting the air, he replied, "I do not know, my young friend, but I think it would be wise for us to keep our distance if we should happen to stumble upon some more."

Therseus plucked a blade of grass. Chewing on its end, he was surprised to find it sweet, not unlike honey. "How much farther till we cross this plain?"

Loekor replied, "A half-day's walking should put us on the

fringe of the Blue Forest. We will make a camp there tonight." He stood, shouldered the pack, and started the half-day's walk with Therseus in close pursuit, awed by his friend's stamina.

At the end of the day, with the sun casting long shadows on the ground, the two stood on a high bluff overlooking a small valley that they would have to cross to enter the forest beyond.

Therseus, standing on the edge of the bluff, exclaimed, "By the laws, it is blue as is the grass that covers the valley floor."

Loekor left the rim of the bluff in search of wood for the evening fire, leaving Therseus to stare in wonder at the spectacle laid out before him. He watched the grass undulate in the evening breeze, as the red sun sunk on the horizon, causing a darker hue to come to the trees as they stood majestically in their stead. He watched the river turn from yellow to a burnished gold, as it slowly wound its way through the valley on its unknown destination. Tearing his eyes away from the view, he turned, sighed, and left the edge of the bluff to help Loekor gather wood.

The two did not go unnoticed as they stood on the edge of the high bluff, overlooking the valley and forest below. The large, bird-like creature extended its wings, which were covered in green scales. Blinking its large, yellow eyes, it debated going after the prey which had so carelessly showed itself. Looking up into the large red disk of the slowly sinking sun, it quickly diminished any thought of an early dinner, for it was a nocturnal creature.

Over the evening fire, while roasting the birds Therseus had shot earlier that day, proud of his marksmanship with the bow he carried, he asked, "Have you ever been to the Blue Forest before?" He stared at Loekor with a look of expectation.

"No, I never have," he answered, while turning the birds so they might roast evenly. He looked across at Therseus, clearly seeing the disappointment registered on his face. "But there are people in my tribe that have."

Hearing this, Therseus leaned forward with all his attention focused on Loekor. "What did they see in this strange forest?"

Loekor sat back looking up into the sky as if searching for words.

Therseus's voice brought him out of his thoughts.

"Loekor," he paused, "I asked, what kind of animals may be

found in the Blue Forest?"

Stirring the coals around in the fire, going back to his childhood, he dredged the memories from his mind. "It has been a long time, my young friend. I was a young buck when these stories were told around the campfires of my home. I do recall something about a huge bird though. Let me see. . . Yes, I remember now. They said there was a large, bird-like creature with large yellow eyes that seemed to glow. It was covered in scales like a fish and had great talons that were so powerful they could squeeze you into two pieces. But the worst thing about this creature was what it ate." He noticed Therseus's eyes were growing round, and his mouth was hanging slightly ajar. "It feasted on flesh such as ours. There are other creatures just as fierce, and would surely kill you if given the chance, but of these I don't remember too well." Therseus shuddered at the thought of these nightmare creatures residing in such close proximity to their camp.

"But listen when I say we will have to keep a wary eye for the untrodden paths we take on the morrow." So saying, he returned his attention to the birds roasting and emitting a pleasant aroma.

Therseus wondered why Loekor would want to travel to such a dangerous place, but then he thought, "Where else would one find evil?" Giving himself to Loekor's wisdom, he laid back, thinking of the foul creatures they might meet on the morrow.

After eating their evening meal, they decided it would be wise to take turns standing watch so that nothing might surprise them while they slept. Loekor went to the edge of the bluff after walking the perimeter of their small camp and gazed up into the night sky. He saw the full moon casting its green rays down on the land. Looking toward the east, he noticed the full moon's light gave the forest an ethereal appearance, as if it were twilight. As he looked out over the forest, he noticed a large winged creature had taken to the air and was rapidly ascending into the cool night. He turned and walked back to the small fire, which was still burning, and kicked dirt over it, dousing it. He didn't want a confrontation with the winged creature. Looking over to Therseus, who was sleeping soundly, he decided not to wake him as he made his way to the edge of the bluff and watched the winged creature's progress as it circled the forest, searching for prey.

Therseus woke with the dawn, and seeing Loekor sitting on the bluff, he walked over to sit beside his friend. "Why did you not wake me?" Asking this, Therseus turned and caught his breath as his eyes took in the sight before him.

"I felt no need to wake you, as I could not sleep anyway." Loekor could see the way Therseus's eyes lit up, seeing the forest, and he thought, "Beware, my young friend, this beauty is deceptive."

Therseus started down into the valley, looking at the blue grass as the wind blew across its velvety surface, causing it to undulate, giving it the appearance of deep blue water. He stared as if in expectation of seeing it spill its bounty upon the ground, but instead, it beckoned him closer, as if wanting to draw him into its depths so it could smother him with its beauty.

Loekor placed a large hand on his shoulder, causing Therseus to blink rapidly as it brought him out of his almost hypnotic reverie. "We should break camp, young friend, and try to find a trail or path leading down."

It didn't take long to find a small path, but who, or what had made it, they had no idea. They slowly treaded their way down with no mishaps to finally stand on the valley floor.

"It is beautiful," Therseus said. "The grass is a lot taller than what I thought, though."

Loekor looked thoughtful as he placed one cloven hoof into the boundaries of the grass and, finding the ground solid, he nodded his head in silent approval. "Keep close," he said. "It would be easy to lose one's companion here."

They made their way through the grass, not being able to see what was in front of them for the first hundred yards or so. Gradually, it thinned out enough for them to see ten yards, sometimes more, as they cautiously made their way. As the grass thinned, they saw what appeared to be small reptilian creatures, but before they could make a closer inspection of them, they would dart down a hole.

"What kind of animal do you think they are?" asked Therseus in a hushed whisper, not wanting to disturb the quiet around them.

"I would be afraid to guess," answered Loekor. "Whatever they are, they seem harmless enough."

"They kind of remind me of a rabbit," said Therseus. "But with that rough brown hide, it would surely disqualify them for this. Look, there's one now!"

Loekor followed his pointing finger and saw one of the strange creatures standing on its hind legs and scenting the air as it twitched its ears that were easily twice as long as its body. Making a loud clucking sound, it disappeared into the hole it had been guarding.

"Wonder what..." Therseus grew silent as the two travelers heard a loud snorting behind them that reverberated in their ears. The two looked at each other, and without saying a word, made a headlong dash for what they hoped was safety. As they ran, they could feel the ground vibrating below them as the beast advanced.

Bursting from the grass, they almost stumbled into the river that they had seen from the bluff, running swifter than what they had at first thought, as it flowed past them with debris it had claimed from the steep banks bordering its sides. Not wanting to chance the currents or the denizens that might lurk below its surface, Loekor lowered his head, brandishing his horns and waiting for the charge of the beast he was sure would soon be crashing through the grass. His keen peripheral vision saw Therseus fumbling with his bow as he nervously notched the arrow to his bowstring, bracing his legs as he did so.

Surprise etched itself across their faces when the inevitable charge was not forthcoming. Relaxing their battle-ready stance, they searched the brush in front of them. They tensed as a loud snorting rend the air, as they witnessed tufts of grass and dirt being flung violently into the air amid the squeals of what they guessed to be the smaller creature's death throes.

"I think we are lucky," Therseus said, lowering his bow. "The beast found something else to vent its hunger on." Turning, he looked at the river rushing past him.

"Yes, I think you are right." Luck, Loekor thought, while also turning to the river, scanning its banks.

The small shelled aquatic creature, seeing movement on one of the lower parts of the bank, tentatively extended one of its several tentacles, covered with thousands of small yellow suction cups, and investigated what it hoped was food. Feeling the warmth from its prey, it encircled the ankle with a tenacious grip but found it quickly disengaged, which caused it great distress as it extended more tentacles to grope along the muddy surface of the bank.

"Did you see that?" asked Therseus, recoiling from the strange appendage which was even now searching for him. Looking at the orange tentacle, a feeling of revulsion came over him, causing an involuntary shiver. Seeing more of the tentacles surfacing and finding their way to the bank, he stepped forward and stamped down hard on two of them. Hearing a squishing sound, he let a smile of satisfaction crease his face. "That will teach you to pick on someone your own size, water demon."

Loekor, witnessing this display of courage on Therseus' part, reached out and pulled him away from the bank, where he himself stared fascinated at what Therseus had called a water demon.

"We had better go downriver to find a shallow place to ford," said Loekor, "I don't want to find out if this water beast has bigger relatives." He turned and started walking down the bank, careful not to get too close to the water but also trying to keep his distance from the tall blue grass. He felt very vulnerable. He was surprised to hear Therseus whistling a tune. Glancing over his shoulder, he noticed Therseus walking behind him, careful to stay within his tracks. "A smart lad," Loekor thought.

Within a short time, they found a shallow place to cross the river, and testing the bottom by prodding it with a stick, they crossed; they felt a rush of relief wash over them. Standing on the threshold of the Blue Forest, they stared in wonder at these silent monoliths.

"Are they not grand?" asked Therseus.

"Yes, yes they are," answered Loekor in a quiet voice, feeling as if he had been here before, even if it had been only in a dream.

Therseus leaned his head back to see the tops of the trees which seemed to tickle the bottom of the reddish sky, as a sigh escaped him. Seeing the oblong fleshy leaves of the trees brought him memories of just how far he was from his own homeland and what a strange quest he had embarked on. Reaching out, he ran his hand over the tree's bark and found it cold and smooth, without a blemish to mar its surface. "It is truly a magical place," he thought.

Loekor's voice drifted over to shake him out of his quiet reverence. "They are truly exquisite, my young friend, but let us make haste. We must find shelter before nightfall."

As they traveled through the forest, they could perceive sounds of rustling from the branches towering above their heads. Once they stopped to look up, and saw a small furry animal with large eyes glaring down at them from one of the tall branches, forming a canopy above their heads. It started chattering, what they guessed to be insults from their intrusion upon what it considered to be its domain. Making apologies to the strange animal, they continued on, with the chattering growing distant in their ears.

A few miles brought them to an open clearing. The sound of running water came to them, and following its singing to the quiet forest around it, they came upon a small spring which gurgled happily, as if welcoming the two travelers.

"This is strange," remarked Theseus as he knelt to put his hand in the red-colored water and tasted the small drops that had accumulated on his fingers. "It is as sweet as the wine you carry, Loekor."

Loekor also knelt, tasted the water, and came away with the same conclusion. "I have heard stories of this water from the village elders of my tribe. I must confess, I did not believe it existed. They say it will restore your vitality, and after seeing this with my own eyes, who am I to cast doubt on their wisdom?"

They made camp that night in the small clearing with the spring serenading them, as it bubbled up over the rocks surrounding it. Sleep had trouble finding them, though, with the sounds of night beasts growling and snarling so close at hand.

CHAPTER FOUR

The Cloud and the Scepter

With the coming of dawn, the night sounds diminished. As the sun rose to herald in the new day, the night sounds quit completely, to be replaced by an almost eerie quietness.

Sitting up, Therseus looked toward the forest that had caused so much unease the night before and chuckled to himself. "As bad as a child seeing haunts in every corner," he thought to himself as the sun's rays broke through the rich cover of light blue leaves to play on the forest floor. Standing up, he felt an air of tranquility as dust motes emerged from the forest floor to dance on the sun's warm rays, giving it a rainbow of colors as they slowly spiraled through the air on their unknown migration. "How could such beauty hold any evil?" he thought, while admonishing himself for last night's fears.

The day beckoned him with a promise of fair weather, as the sun continued its slow climb to its preordained place to shine down on this small world, covering it with its life-giving warmth. The young man felt almost joy at finding a new, although unusual friend, the beautiful day that awaited him, and the adventure that awaited them both. With these thoughts playing through his mind, he basked in the sun greedily, luxuriating in its warmth as it quickly dispelled the night's chilly dampness. He found himself at peace with the world around him until a dark cloud crept into his mind and whispered into his subconscious of the reason he was here; these new thoughts quickly alleviated the happiness he had only seconds earlier. Tears of frustration sprang to his eyes as he remembered the quiet summer days in his village, of frolicking with the village's unattached girls and lazily swimming in the clear lake found deep in the forest of his homeland, and no thoughts but those of the next hunt entered to range upon his mind. As these thoughts came, a helpless rage stole over him. "Why?" he asked in a voice full of tormented emotion as he looked to the heavens, as if expecting his answer from above, but instead, hearing his own voice echo back at him from the tall trees surrounding the clearing. "Do you mock me?" he asked, feeling the anger pouring out of him but not able to control it, as he stood with arms hanging by his sides as he clenched and unclenched his hands. Spent, he dropped to his knees; a small sob escaped him at the hopelessness of the quest he had set before himself.

    Loekor, an unwilling witness to his friend's emotions, turned from the trail he had been following back to their camp after foraging for food, to give the young man a few minutes to find and compose himself. He felt his own heart tugging at him and his eyes watering as his heart went out to the young friend he had found so recently. "You will have your revenge, young friend. Of that, I am sure." He turned and made his way back to their camp, whistling as he did so, to warn Therseus of his coming.

    "Ho, I see you are awake," said Loekor, putting on an air of joviality in hope of raising the young man's spirits. "It will be a fine day for travel, will it not?"

    "I guess it will," answered Therseus in a somber mood.

    Loekor, upon seeing his friend's dark depression, said, "Do not fear; we will find whatever it was that has visited this darkness on your village. We will deal severely with this evil and then free the people of your village."

    If they still be alive, Therseus thought to himself.

    "Come, let us eat before we venture further."

    A small green cloud with small amber sparks revolving in its depths glided toward the two travelers unnoticed until it was almost upon them. A high-pitched scratchy voice came from the cloud, causing the two travelers to leap from the ground to turn and stare in open-mouthed wonder at the strange apparition that presented itself before them, floating scant inches above the ground.

    "What do you hear at the forest of Kronus?" After asking this, the cloud shifted shape and moved closer, causing Therseus to take a backward step, almost tripping over the fire.

"I come in search of the witch that lives in this forest on a matter of great urgency. I fear," answered Loekor, standing his ground but feeling his stomach knot in nervous anticipation.

"And of what nature does this urgency of yours pertain to?"

Loekor ran his tongue over his dry lips, wondering if he should divulge his information. The Dark One has many minions, he reminded himself. "This matter is for the telling to the witch, and none else. Our intentions toward her are honorable. We seek her advice, not to do harm."

The small cloud drifted over to Therseus who had remained silent during this exchange. Continually changing shape, the cloud circled around him as if it was inspecting the young man. Therseus wanted to run from this apparition but could see no avenue of escape as his eyes darted around while trying to keep the cloud in front of him. He looked to Loekor with a silent plea on his face.

Before Loekor could speak, the cloud shape asked, "I see that you travel with a youth. Is this all?"

"It is all," Loekor replied. "We are but two travelers."

The voice in the cloud seemed to think on this before it spoke again. "Are you not afraid of the beasts that lurk in this forest?"

"We would be fools not to be wary," answered Loekor. "But there are worse things in this world to be afraid of. Of that, I am sure you are well aware."

Therseus looked from the cloud to Loekor, emotions fighting within him. He could not leave his friend to defend himself from whatever lurked in this cloud. He resigned himself to this and waited for what might happen.

"As much as I like conversation, my mysterious visitor, I find it more enjoyable to know who it is I am addressing," said Loekor. "Especially if they are to be found in my camp. I hope you will forgive me for my brusqueness. I must confess it is not one of my better virtues, but it has served me well over the years."

"So be it." At these words, the cloud slowly dissipated to reveal an old bent woman no more than three feet tall.

The two travelers could not hide the surprise that showed plainly on their faces.

The woman was dressed in a blue robe that all but covered her tiny figure. The wrinkles lining her face showed her as very old, almost ancient, but they did not disguise the beauty that had once resided there. She looked out at Loekor with lively dancing blue eyes. She could sense the eyes of Therseus glued on her back and did not bother to turn around as she said, "What are you gawking at, youngster? Have you never seen a witch?"

Therseus could feel goosebumps rising on his arms and legs. "She must have eyes in the back of her head," he thought as he walked over to station himself beside Loekor.

Loekor smiled, bowed and asked, "May I present myself?"

"You may," she replied, steadying her gaze on Therseus whom she guessed to be no more than eighteen summers old.

"I am Loekor, King of the Horned Ones that dwell in the Yellow Forest of Pandasia and this young man is my traveling companion and ally. Therseus, from the Green Forest of Man."

Therseus's eyes grew wide at hearing this, but he decided it best to keep his silence, although his new admiration for Loekor was evident in the new stance he took as he squared his shoulders and stood straighter beside his friend, hoping it would befit the king that had so recently emerged from its hiding place. He wondered why Loekor had not entrusted him with this information to begin with. It was probably for the best, he thought. How could a hunter and woodsman be expected to act around a king?

Mayhap you be the one I have waited for these many years. The old witch thought to herself, "Perhaps you are the one," hiding her excitement from them. She turned to re-enter the forest; the cloud reappeared to swirl around her feet and soon climbed to cover her completely. "It remains to be seen. Follow me." Saying this, she glided swiftly over the ground, finally coming to rest beside the edge of the trees. "Make haste," she called back, impatience sounding in her voice.

The two followed the cloud through the dense trees and soon found themselves deep in the forest, trusting the small witch to guide them safely to wherever they were traveling to.

The cloud gradually slowed its pace to allow Loekor and Therseus a chance to recuperate from their exertions. Therseus was wearying to the point of exhaustion, although he tried hard not to show this. Therseus felt a hand on his shoulder and looked up to see Loekor smiling down on him, giving him silent encouragement.

At last the cloud came to rest by a large tree, larger than those that shared its company and by contrast, a much darker hue than its brethren. As the cloud evaporated, the old woman put a gnarled hand on the tree's smooth trunk, causing a door to silently slide open and beckoned the two travelers enter.

Loekor glanced around the forest, testing the air before entering with Therseus in tow. Adjusting their eyes to the room's gloomy interior, they jumped as a fire started in the small hearth without aid.

The witch returned from an adjoining room carrying a tray. "I hope my hospitality serves you well. It has been a very long time since I have occasioned to have a visitor here. I'm sure you will find this wine very palatable. It is well aged, of that I can assure you." Saying this, she handed Loekor and Therseus goblets encrusted with gems.

Loekor tasted the wine and indeed found it very palatable and surprisingly very refreshing as he felt it coursing its way through his body, giving it new vigor. Studying the goblet, he noticed runes inscribed upon its surface but did not question this, not wanting to take a chance at agitating his host who was watching him with more than just a casual eye.

Therseus, seeing no ill effect on his friend from the wine, tentatively took a sip and also found it very tasty and refreshing. He turned the goblet up and finished its contents in two swallows, feeling the wine's warmth spreading from his stomach to his limbs.

"Will you not share my fire?" asked the witch from across the room.

Crossing the room, they sat on two stools they were sure were not there seconds ago.

The witch pulled a blue cloak about her and sat hunched by the fire in an ornately carved chair as she stared intently at Loekor, as if trying to see into his very being. Loekor returned her stare with a slight grin playing loosely on his face. "You were right about the wine, my dear lady. It was indeed very refreshing."

"It serves two purposes, my horned one," she answered.

"And what might they be, if I may be so bold as to ask?"

A cackle escaped her lips before she answered, startling Therseus, who was at the moment in a euphoric mood caused by the wine as it played upon his system. "It is a very old wine. It was made by the very elves that used to live in this forest. It has great restorative powers unless it is consumed by one of the dark one's minions or the dark one himself. Whereas it would quickly reduce them to a smoldering heap. As you can see from your young friend, it has a very quieting effect on mere mortals."

Loekor noticed Therseus starting to sway from side to side and after obtaining a silent agreement from the witch, he gently laid Therseus down in front of the fire so that he might slumber in comfort.

"It is well that the young one sleeps, for the tale I'm going to tell you is not for mortal ears."

"Am I not a mortal?" asked Loekor, resuming his seat so that he might face the witch across from him.

"It is a very good question you put to me," said the witch as she turned her gaze toward the fire. "I'm afraid the only answer I may give is; yes and no."

"I do not understand," replied Loekor, his brow creasing in thought.

"You will in time, my horned one," she said. "You will in time. I will tell you this much; though you can be hurt and bleed like any mortal, and quite possibly die, you are endowed with special powers, which will come to you when the time is ripe. I am sorry, but this is all I may reveal to you at this time. It is for your own safety, believe me. As for myself, as I'm sure you've already guessed; I will help you on this dark journey you must make. It will be west, always west."

"May I ask you the reason for all of this?" asked Loekor, sitting on the edge of the stool with his hands clasped in front of him.

The witch leaned back, pulling her cloak tighter around her small frame, as she let her thoughts go back to the past. Taking a deep breath, she began her story. "It started a thousand years ago with the goblin wars. Men and elves fought side by side against this evil tide that threatened to destroy this fragile world. But wait, I'm getting ahead of myself. Have you ever heard of a great wizard by the name of Soren?"

Furrowing his brow in thought, Loekor answered, "It is a name that escapes me."

"Even the legends die," she said, letting a heavy sigh escape her. "I will tell you, he was probably the greatest wizard that has yet lived on this world. Some have said he was as old as this forest, maybe older. Of this, I cannot be sure. Before the goblin wars, he disappeared entrusting his magical scepter to the elvish kind, with a promise to hold it for him until his return. Of the journey he took, no one had any idea. Soon after he vanished, the goblins took it upon themselves to make war on elves and man alike. I am not sure what prompted this, but I think it may have had something to do with Soren's disappearance. As long as Soren walked this world, peace reigned, for evil would not dare rear its ugly head in this wizard's presence. But alas, he did vanish, and the goblins took advantage of this, attacking without warning, destroying thousands of mortals and elves alike before they could retaliate. In a small village not far from here, they stole the scepter that had been secreted there for protection against this very act. The goblins who were very crafty beings outsmarted themselves when they evoked the dark one from his vile resting place with the scepter." She paused, taking another deep breath before continuing. "He soon made slaves of the goblins as well as invoking his own dark minions from that most vile and unholy place. He was almost unstoppable as he unleashed his dark powers, using the scepter to magnify these powers tenfold. It took every witch and wizard on this planet to thwart his evil spells. For a hundred years, this war was waged, costing countless lives, mortal and immortal. The final battle was fought on Mount Kan, which was a fiery volcano at the time. The elves' king, Klonan, fought bravely against the dark one and seeing he was losing, grabbed the scepter and threw himself to a fiery death. Without the scepter, we were able to bind the dark one with spells and cast him into a cave we sealed from whence he came. Without his leadership what few goblins remained escaped and have not been seen since, though I am sure they are still out there somewhere waiting as his minions are."

"Why now?" asked Loekor. "Why after all these years?"

"This I cannot answer my horned one," she replied. "Maybe the dark one feels it is time. Maybe he feels he can win this time. There are very few witches left and even fewer wizards to oppose him."

"And what of the elves?"

"After the last battle, they banned themselves from the world of man. You must understand, they were very bitter over losing their king and I suppose this was their self-punishment. On the morrow, we start our journey to enlist the aid of the elves."

"And what if they choose not to join us?"

"Then I am afraid it is possible we would be cast in an evil shadow that would encircle this world for a thousand years," said the witch, staring into the small fire with the flames' dancing lights reflecting off her face. "Then we must not let this happen," intoned Loekor.

"We must gather our forces before the dark one can locate the scepter; it is the only way," said the witch.

"Would it not be best to leave now?" asked Loekor.

"The night belongs to the dark one; it would be unwise. You must be careful Loekor, for you are the chosen."

"The chosen..." Echoed Loekor, growing quiet as he contemplated this information.

"Yes, my horned one, the chosen," said the witch. "The dark one and his minions will be watching for you. We rest tonight, for I fear this will be the last night we may rest safe from the dark one."

They did not hear the rustle of wings or the cackle that emitted from the foul creature's mouth as the harpy took wing to report to its dark master. It would be well rewarded this night for the information it now possessed. The harpy was borne high above the Blue Forest on the wings of darkness. Flying a westward course, it spied the object it sought. The Black Mountain rose high above the desolate landscape that surrounded it, with its black twisted trees bearing bitter fruit. The harpy started its spiraling downward dive that would lead it to the cavern's opening and the dark one that waited within.

CHAPTER FIVE

The Seer's Warning

The young elf king sat in the gilded chair, listening half-heartedly to his chief adviser as he let his eyes rove around the torch-lit hall. He watched the shadows dance on the wooden walls, carved with ancient symbols of his ancestors. He felt bored and restless, longing for something more exciting than endless reports and councils.

"It is true, King Illson," said Aeso, Chief Adviser to the King of Elves. His voice was grave and urgent. "Maloc the Seer has reported strange happenings around the Black Mountain. He has seen signs of comings and goings, of dark magic and foul creatures."

"And what am I to do?" asked the king, as he daintily picked his teeth with a sliver of wood. He sounded weary and annoyed. "What army am I supposed to raise to reconquer this menace? Was my father's life not enough?"

The chief adviser could feel his indignation rising, as the king's indifference swept over him. He clenched his fists and leaned forward. "My young lord, we must make haste and send runners to gather our forces and allies. We cannot ignore this threat any longer. The Dark One is rising again."

The king sighed and set down his goblet of wine. He looked at his adviser with a cold and skeptical gaze. "And if we march against this dark evil you speak of, what are we to do about guarding our small kingdom from the Dark Elves? Our army is pitifully small. I see no way we can split our forces and go to war with this legend, this Dark One you speak of, and still hold this kingdom from the Dark

Elves. They have been waging war against us since I was but a small babe. This threat, adviser, is one that I can taste and feel, not a thousand-year-old ghost that may or may not even exist." He paused and took another sip of wine, waiting for his adviser's what he knew would be a curt reply.

"It is no jest, my lord, when I speak of the Dark One," said Aeso, his voice trembling with emotion. "This threat is very real. Ask any of your warriors that were there during the Hundred Year War. I'm sure the memory is as fresh as if it had happened only hours ago. Your brave father made the ultimate sacrifice to be rid of this evil. Have you not read the scrolls of Linen?"

The chief adviser paced the floor, waiting for his young lord's answer. He wished the king could have seen what he had seen on that dark and bloody day, when his father fell to the Dark One's blade. He wished the king could feel the urgency and the danger that loomed over their realm.

"Let me think on this today," said the young king, rising from his chair. "I will summon you this evening to give you my answer." He walked towards a small door leading to his private chambers, leaving his adviser behind.

"Time is of the essence, my young lord," called Aeso to his king's retreating back. He muttered under his breath, "Young fool." He quickly admonished himself for thinking this. He respected and loved his king, but he also feared for his fate. "If only your father were here," he thought, as he turned to leave the hall on errands he was sure King Illson would greatly disapprove of.

Leaving the small palace, Aeso trudged through the backstreets of the kingdom, amid the stares of his fellow elves. They knew him as the chief adviser, but they also knew him as a rebel and a conspirator. He had made many enemies among the nobles and the courtiers, who resented his influence and his boldness.

He stopped at the entrance to a stone dwelling, hidden among the alleys and shops. He knocked three times on the wooden door and announced himself. The door opened with a creak and he entered the dim room with a fire burning in its center.

An old elf dressed in a dark lavender robe hunched over the fire, feeding it with herbs that caused a sweetish odor to pervade the room. He was Maloc the Seer, Aeso's oldest friend and ally. He had been the one who had warned Aeso of the Dark One's return, based on his visions and prophecies.

"I see that you have returned, Aeso," he said, not taking his eyes from the fire. "What did our king say on this matter of grave importance that you delivered to him?"

"I fear he is slow to heed my advice," answered Aeso. He felt a pang of frustration and disappointment.

"I expected as much," said Maloc, rising to fetch a flagon of wine and goblets. He handed one to Aeso and gestured for him to sit down on a cushioned bench. "I have some more news, but first, I think it would be wise for us to quench our parched throats, old friend."

Tasting the wine, Aeso raised his eyebrows, looking over the rim of the goblet at his friend. "This wine has an unusual flavor, not at all like the elvish brew I've had of late."

"It was but a token payment from the witch Klonel," said Maloc with a sly smile. "I helped her dispose of a small problem not many days ago." He sipped the wine, appreciating its strange flavor. "I hope it will be our secret. I do not think it would be looked on kindly if I accepted payment from Klonel. She is not well-liked among our people. She has a reputation for meddling with dark forces and forbidden arts. The elves and witches are not the best of friends these days, but that will soon have to change, I fear," said Maloc, his voice low and serious.

Aeso stopped midway from taking a drink, to stare at his friend, upon hearing this. He felt a surge of curiosity and apprehension. What had Maloc seen in his visions that made him say such a thing?

"Here, here, my friend, let us finish this fine wine, before I relate to you what I have seen," said Maloc, noticing Aeso's reaction. He returned his attention to the wine, savoring the bouquet that assailed his sense of smell.

Aeso sipped his wine while staring at the tapestries that were the only decorations adorning the walls in the simple room. He felt a catch in his throat while looking at the scenes depicted on the tapestries' velvety surface: elves at play and working together in harmony and peace. He remembered those days, before the Dark One came and shattered their world. "If only time could move backward," he thought. "It would be a far better world. If not for the Dark One." He clenched the goblet until his knuckles turned white at this last thought.

"Something disturbs you, my friend," said Maloc, noticing the grip Aeso had on the goblet.

"I am sorry, old friend, but I have a habit of late of letting the past seep into my thoughts as I think on the future," said Aeso. He set the goblet down and stared intently at the old elf sitting across from him.

"Yes, they were better days," said Maloc with a sigh. "Did we not have the most beautiful cities in all of this world?" He also set his goblet down and looked at Aeso with a sad smile. "I have tried many times to see if this may be so again, but a dark cloud settles over my vision, obscuring this from me."

"Mayhap it is the Dark One causing this," said Aeso as he got up to pace the clay-tiled floor. "If only the king would heed my warning. Although I must confess; I know not what advice I would give him even if he did decide to take action." He stopped his pacing and paused in his speech. He looked expectantly at the seer with a look of dread on his face, as if afraid of the answer his friend would give him. "I was...I was hoping you might help me on this, old friend."

Maloc stood up and clasped his friend's arm in a warm embrace. "Do not fear, Aeso, for the answer to your question is coming from an unexpected quarter." He reseated himself and beckoned his friend to follow suit. After Aeso was again seated, he related what he had seen in the flames. "As of this moment, three travelers are coming to seek our help and alliance. We must not turn them down in this."

"Only three?" asked Aeso, incredulity sounding in his voice. "Of what help can they be?"

Maloc smiled at his friend as he reached over to lay his hand on his friend's arm. "Of the three, one of them is well known to the elves." Maloc saw he had his friend's undivided attention. "It is the witch of the Blue Forest, Cassis."

"What!" said Aeso, jumping to his feet. "I thought she met her demise at the end of the goblin wars."

"No, it is true, old friend. Even now, she journeys here with her two companions." He poured more wine into his goblet before continuing. "It is up to you to make sure she receives the welcome she deserves."

"You can rest assured on that," said Aeso, feeling a surge of hope and curiosity. Cassis was a legend among the elves, a powerful and mysterious witch who had helped them in their darkest hour. He wondered who her companions were and what they wanted. "Is there anything else you might tell me?" he asked.

"Yes, but first sample a little more of this wine. It has a calming effect," said Maloc, noticing his friend's excitement. He handed him another goblet and waited for him to drink. "You must locate the leader of the Dark Elves and enlist his aid."

Aeso opened his mouth to speak, but only a gurgling ensued as the wine dribbled forgotten from his mouth. He coughed and cleared his throat. "Would it not be better for me to cut my own throat! Surely the Dark Elves would skewer me with arrows before I could get close enough to speak. Have you forgotten what happened the last time we sent a messenger of peace?" He remembered the gruesome fate of the envoy who had been sent back in pieces as a warning. He drained the goblet, letting the sweet nectar rush down his throat. It spread its warmth to his limbs, causing a slight heaviness to settle on his frame.

Maloc could not help the dour amusement he felt as he watched his friend down the wine in a single gulp. "Easy, old friend, for that wine you drink takes a bit of getting used to. And do not fear, for I do not see your death in the near future. I am so sure of this that I choose to go with you on your search for the leader of these so-called Dark Elves. If my sight does not deceive me, we will find them in the hills north of here." He rose and embraced his friend. "Now, I must rest, for this seeing is very tiring. I hope you will excuse me."

Emerging from the stone dwelling, Aeso stared up into the sky, squinting his eyes against the sun's glare. He walked back to the palace, the way he had come, through the dirty garbage-strewn backstreets with stone and clay buildings looming on either side of the cobbled street. "Where has our pride gone?" he asked himself, remembering the cities of white and gold with their spires reaching toward the heavens.

Picking his way through the narrow passages of the street, he soon found himself in the central square of the kingdom, where peddlers were plying their trade in loud hawking voices. He looked at the peddlers with disgust written plainly on his features. "Have we sunk so low!" he thought. "So like the mortals we've condemned and despised these thousand years." Reaching the center of the square, he paused to dip his hand in the cool water found in the large ornate fountain decorating the drab square. The fountain was carved with images of elves and animals living in harmony. It was one of the few reminders of their glorious past. He wiped the grime and dirt away that had accumulated on his face during his short sojourn to see his friend Maloc. Satisfied, he readjusted his canary yellow cape (which was a sign of his office) and stared around once more with disdain at his fellow elves as he continued his short trek to the palace and the offices that awaited him. He could hear the murmur of the peddlers and their customers as he pushed his way through. He barely acknowledged the guards who stood at rigid attention in their bright green leathers as he finally entered the security of the palace. He was surprised to find the palace empty and decided to take advantage of the quiet solitude to meditate on the problem that had so recently presented itself.

Across the small kingdom, a meeting was taking place in a hidden cave. "Have you talked to the Chief Adviser?" asked the young elf who was dressed entirely in black. He looked around nervously, as if expecting an attack at any moment.

"Yes," answered Maloc. "He will meet with your leader. And remember, he must not be harmed in any way. We must put aside our petty grievances, at least until the Dark One is disposed of." He stood waiting for the young elf he knew only as Lark to guarantee him and Aeso safe passage.

"My lord agrees with you, Seer, and will guarantee you and the King's Chief Adviser a safe journey to and from our camp. When will you come?" He asked, hearing an outside noise and reaching for his dagger that adorned his thick leather belt. But the noise subsided. It was only a bat flying by.

"We must wait for the King's answer on the morrow, so we will know what plan of action to take. If he realizes the magnitude of the Dark One's threat, then mayhap he will see the wisdom of calling a truce, so that our armies may join forces." He pulled his robe tighter around himself as the night's chilly dampness entered the cave.

"So be it, Seer." Looking out the cave entrance, the young elf silently slipped into the night, to become one with its shadows.

Maloc huddled closer to the fire, hoping Aeso would forgive his deceit. "It is the only way, old friend," he thought. "There are great forces on the move, light as well as dark." Reaching into his robe, he produced a small leather bag and proceeded to sprinkle its contents into the fire. He waited for the vision that had eluded him on previous occasions. With a small hissing noise, a dull gray smoke appeared over the fire. As Maloc looked on, a darker shape surfaced in the cloud. Gradually the darker shape took the form of a head; and finally, a grim malevolent face appeared to scorn the Seer. It bared its long canine teeth in a mockery of a smile. Maloc jumped up, kicking at the fire and scattering the embers across the tiled floor. The vision disintegrated. "It is no use," he said aloud in frustration as he reached for the goblet of wine he had poured earlier and downed it quickly. He thought, "I will catch you asleep soon, Dark One." He thought he heard a hoarse laughter in his small chamber, but decided it must have been his imagination. Still, it sent a tingle up his spine to tickle the base of his neck.

In his offices, Aeso pondered the trouble with the elves and their division. It had started soon after King Klonan's demise, when he threw himself and the scepter of magic into the volcano to ensure the scepter's disappearance from the world. Proclaiming his young son heir to the elvish throne had separated the elves into two factions. One faction stood behind the young king, while the other wanted an older and wiser elf to sit upon the throne. They had built this small kingdom in a land almost completely surrounded by a swamp for the young king to rule in peace, while the other elves chose to live in the hills to the north. How they had come to be known as the Dark Elves, Aeso never knew; although he thought, "Maybe this evil Maloc speaks of will bring the elves together again under one rule."

CHAPTER SIX

The Kingdom of Elves: A Divided Realm

Lark silently made his way through the dark, winding streets until he came upon the high stone wall that surrounded the small kingdom. Searching in the weeds, he recovered the rope and grappling hook that enabled him to scale the wall without arousing the guards that patrolled the perimeter around the heavy gate leading into the kingdom. Climbing the wall, he perched on top, staring back the way he had come to make sure there was no pursuit as he dropped silently to the other side. Crouching against the wall, he perceived movement to his right as other figures dressed in black stepped out from their well-concealed hiding places. The biggest of these stepped forward to clap Lark on the shoulder, welcoming him back before turning to re-enter the bushes that had concealed them from view. The others in the small group followed silently in his wake, as quietly as a jungle cat stalking its prey on soft padded paws.

    They traveled many miles from the kingdom before any word was uttered. This was not before they reached the outermost fringe of the hills that dotted the landscape they called home. Building a small fire and banking its sides so as not to attract attention from curious eyes, they spitted hares the group had snared earlier that evening. Sitting in a tight huddled group, they discussed the preparations they would make as the rabbits roasted on the spits.

    "So," said Grimdom, the biggest of the lot. "Maloc agrees then."

    "Yes," answered Lark. "The Dark One's forces are gathering even now as we speak. It was luck we got away from the goblin patrol unscathed, and even more so when we were able to follow them to the mountain of the Dark One's tomb without being spotted. It is as it was a thousand years ago." He paused, staring into the fire before he spoke again to the silent audience seated around the fire, waiting for his next words. "I just hope Maloc, with the Chief Adviser's help, can convince the young King Illson of the urgency of settling this matter."

"Do they suspect you as the leader of our tribe?" asked Grimdom, turning the spit.

"I am not sure," answered Lark. "But right now, it is of little importance, although I am sure Maloc has suspected this for many years." Saying this, he fell silent, with the only sound being the night creatures as they hunted and died within earshot of the small group.

"Do you believe Cassis is really on her way to the kingdom of elves?" asked Grimdom.

"Yes," answered Lark. "I believe she is, though everyone thought her vanquished on the last day of the Goblin Wars. With her help, I believe we have a chance to be rid of the Dark One, as well as his minions, once and for all. I do not seek peace with the elves who live behind the great walls, just a temporary truce," he said to the tight group. "Living these many years in the bosom of nature has taught me a peace of mind I would be willing to die to preserve. I can never again see myself living in the squalor that the elves behind those walls call home."

Grimdom said, "But would it not be wise to live in harmony with the Kingdom's elves to hunt, fish, and explore the land in peace?" He waited for his leader's reply.

"If you remember, old friend, it was not us who waged this war," answered Lark. "All we ever asked was to be left alone. I do not believe peace will reign between us until the King decrees this, and so far, this has not been done, although his Chief Advisor, Aeso, has tried to persuade him in this." Taking a deep breath, he went on. "Was it not the very messenger Aeso sent to us with an offer for peace who warned us of the young king's treachery, of his trap he had laid for us without the Chief Advisor's knowledge?"

"Yes," answered Grimdom. "I remember this well, for that very messenger chose to ally himself with our tribe and even now shares the campfire of our home. A good elf with a bow and arrow."

The big elf grew quiet as he stared across the small space

separating him from Lark and recalled the days of the Goblin Wars. Lark had been a captain in the Royal Guard then, instead of an outcast as he was now. His lean frame hid the strength that lay dormant until the need arose to call it forth. Though his face showed the outward appearance of youth, with dark curly hair crowning it, it was the eyes that drew and held you in their steady gaze. They were quick to show merriment and even quicker to show the berserker that lived behind those placid grey pools. If he had to pick one animal to compare his leader to, he thought, it would have to be the hawk.

"Where do we go from here?" Grimdom asked.

"Nowhere," answered Lark. "We wait here till the morrow and hope Maloc and the Chief Advisor bring us good tidings."

CHAPTER SEVEN
The Elf Alliance

Aeso paced his office anxiously as he waited for the king's summons. He wondered how he would explain what he intended to do. A young elf dressed in silver interrupted his thoughts.

"The king will see you now," the elf said, turning to escort Aeso to the king's apartments.

Entering the apartments, he spied the young king lounging on silken cushions, sipping wine from a golden goblet. The king stared out at him through sky-blue eyes that held a look of innocence. The golden locks adorning his head fell to his shoulders in a haphazard way.

"Come, sit by me, Aeso, so we may talk in private," he said, dismissing the young messenger with a wave of his hand.

Sitting beside the king, Aeso declined the wine offered to him.

"So," asked King Illson, "what did Maloc the Seer have to say about our predicament?"

An angry sigh escaped Aeso. He should have known that word would have reached the king of his visit to Maloc.

King Illson noticed the jaw muscles tightening in Aeso's face as he held back the angry retort that threatened to spew forth. "Do not let this matter trouble you, Aeso. You know as well as I that secrets are not kept in this small kingdom I rule."

He reclined on the cushions, watching the silk-swathed figure before him in great amusement. It was not easy to rile the chief advisor, and he was enjoying the man's discomfort. He remembered the strict rules Aeso had laid before him while he was growing to elfhood.

"I must apologize, Aeso. It's just that the opportunity to make you mad could not go by unnoticed."

"If you were younger, Lord, I surely would make your backside sting for this," said Aeso as he regained his composure.

"I am sure you would. I was not certain you would not punish me anyway, as you did when I was still a babe. Please forgive me for this childishness. I should have more respect for the elf who raised me."

He sipped more of the wine as he tasted the fruits before him and waited for Aeso's report.

Feeling his dignity restored, Aeso related what he had learned from Maloc. "Now it is up to you, Lord. It rests in your hands."

After thinking about this information, the young king replied, "I agree with your wisdom, Aeso. It would be folly not to join forces with the dark elves, but can they be trusted?" It was his turn to wait for the reply, which was shortly forthcoming.

"Of this, I cannot really say, but that is one of the reasons I must meet with the leader of the dark elves. I am sure this same thought plays through his mind. If it can be arranged, I wish to bring him here so that you may assure him there is no treachery involved," said the young king as he raised himself from the cushions and asked, "Will you do this?"

Staring up into the wizened face before him, Aeso replied, "If you think this is right, it will be done. You may tell the leader of the dark elves that there is a truce." He was surprised when the king continued, "and possibly a full pardon when this is over."

"You are showing the true wisdom of a king," said Aeso.

"I had a good teacher," the young king said, smiling up at Aeso. "You said Cassis would arrive on the morrow. Would this not be a good time for a celebration of our forces' reunion?"

"Mayhap I can persuade the dark elves' leader of this," noted Aeso as he returned to his office. He smiled at his good fortune as a springiness returned to his step. He couldn't believe the change of attitude that had been wrought in the young king.

Dressed in warmer clothing, Aeso returned to Maloc's dwelling so that they might go forth in search of the leader of the dark elves. He did not know it had already been arranged.

After Aeso's departure, King Illson sat quietly while thinking about his decision. "I hope I made the right choice," he thought aloud.

He heard a voice coming from the air that said, "You have, my son. Now you are truly the king of the elves." Hearing this, he laid his head down and dozed as a feeling of peace stole over him and wrapped him in its embrace. Before he slept, he felt a touch full of warmth on his forehead that caused him to smile even as sleep overtook him. If he had been awake, he would have noticed the sheer curtains on the window billowing outward as if there was a parting from within the room.

CHAPTER EIGHT
The March of the Goblins

"How much further?" asked the short squat goblin as he tried to keep from dragging his long claw-like hands on the ground. He turned his head so that he might better observe the long scraggly line marching behind him.

"It shouldn't be much further," croaked the leader of this band. He ducked to avoid a low hanging branch. His second in command was not so fortunate. He smacked into the branch, causing a curse to spill from his overly large mouth. He pulled forth the rust-eaten sword and hacked at the branch in a fury of motion as he continued to curse.

The leader turned and hurried back, staying his arm. "Are you crazy? We must not arouse anyone of our presence." Withering under his leader's baleful stare, he re-sheathed the antiquated sword, making no apology. He resumed his place in line while mumbling under his breath.

With darkness cloaking their movement, they soon broke out of the small forest. They gazed upon the dark mountain and its surrounding countryside, presenting a bleak contrast to the forest they had just traveled through. Silently they marched on, with the only sounds being the harsh breathing of the goblins and the clinking of their bits and pieces of armor as their swords bounced against them.

Holding up his arm, the leader halted his long line of goblins in their steady march. "We rest," he croaked. He pointed to two goblins and motioned them to him. "Go to the Black Mountain and see what you might discover. Report back with your findings. We must know if this calling is true."

The two goblins glanced at one another and then slipped silently away, with neither voicing the fear that nibbled at them.

Soon they were close enough to perceive voices coming from the cavern's opening. A dull blue light pulsed from its depths, causing an involuntary shiver to come over them. They squatted behind the sparse brush that dotted the landscape while watching the army of goblins that had already arrived.

"It is almost time," said a deep sonorous voice.

The two goblins froze at the sound of a voice, a frigid fear clutching their hearts. They quickly retraced their steps to their leader, unaware of the harpy circling overhead, watching their every move. Believing themselves unobserved, they stealthily made their way back. However, the harpy wasted no time and flew straight to the cavernous opening to report the goblins' arrival to its dark master.

Perched atop his hellish throne crafted from the bones of his enemies, the Dark One reached down to stroke the harpies filthy head. "And now my foul one, what have you to say?" He leaned back, placing his hands on the thigh bones forming the arms of his throne.

The harpy looked up in adoration and placed its fanged mouth close to the Dark One's ear. It related the activity going on around the mountain.

"Soon, it will be soon," he said to the goblins and other creatures of the night. They shrank back from his baleful stare, his eyes seeming to glow with the evil they mirrored from within. Standing, he threw back his cowled head and laughed. He noticed the goblins cowering in a far corner, which gave him great amusement. He strode to the entrance and looked down on the army of goblins waiting for his orders, willing to die at his bidding.

Walking back to his throne, he turned, reached over his head and clenched his hands as if he was crushing his adversaries. He said, "Our time is almost here. This time we will crush mortals and immortals alike." Raising his voice, he screamed, "Do you hear me?"

"Yes, master," the group chorused, not wanting to displease the large cloaked figure before them. They well knew his displeasure would bring a slow and very painful death. As they looked on, the cloaked figure spread his long tapered fingers, letting a bright blue flame dance between them. He picked a goblin leaning against a far wall and discharged the blue flame in his direction, hitting him squarely in the chest.

The unlucky goblin clawed at his chest, even as the purple skin covering him seared and peeled off. He soon left nothing but a skeleton in its place. A quietness settled over the large cavern as its occupants stood in abject terror, afraid to speak. "Let that be a lesson," he bellowed. "Do not fail me," he roared before resuming his seat upon the grisly throne. Bowing, the congregation quickly emptied from the cavern to rejoin their comrades who waited below. They guarded the human captives they planned to use in finding the lost Scepter of Soren, if it still existed. Though the volcano had collapsed and lost its fiery breath, it would still be almost impossible to locate the scepter no matter how many slaves they used for the task. Though the goblins thought this a foolish gesture on the Dark One's part, they knew what words of protest would bring them.

Before the night was over, the humans found themselves well on their way to Mount Kan with two hundred goblins escorting them. The goblins cursed and lashed them with the small cruel whips they favored and enjoyed using at every opportunity. "Shhhsh... Here they come," whispered the dark-clad figure. He squatted further down behind the small bush and averted his eyes so he would not be staring directly at them, lest he draw their attention. The dark elves took note of the large number of goblins as the line slowly trudged past their position. "Should we attack?" asked one of the numerous elves, stepping out of his hiding place. "No," answered another figure, stepping out and dusting himself off. "We are to scout this region of the Dark One and nothing more." He debated with himself and decided to send two of his scouts back with this information. He and the rest would follow in the goblins' wake. Behind the dark elves, barely a mile away, goblins made their way to the Black Mountain to join their comrades.

CHAPTER NINE

The Swamp Ambush

Loekor, Therseus and Cassis made their way carefully through the treacherous fog-enshrouded swamp. One misguided foot was all it took to become a permanent resident of this bleak and gloomy place. To Therseus, it seemed like weeks had passed since they had entered the swamp.

Plodding along behind his two companions, he thought how nice it would be to have the sun playing on his skin once more. He looked around the grey landscape and heard sucking sounds coming from the shifting mud and sands that made up a large part of the Swamp of No Return. Occasionally he saw a strange form of reptile skittering across the mud on webbed feet, but before he could tell what it might be, it was quickly swallowed by the dense fog that found a home here. Therseus shuddered, keeping an ever watchful eye on the greyness surrounding them.

Coming to a dry place, they decided to halt for a brief rest before continuing. Loekor searched his pack for the herbs he used to brew a kind of tea, while coaxing Therseus to build a small fire.

Banking the fire he had built, Therseus turned and took the pot Loekor offered him. Soon the three were sipping on the strong brew. Therseus found the bitter fluid had a calming effect as the tea brought strength to his overly tired limbs. Soon he grew drowsy and slept, only to be awakened with a start from his brief slumber by Loekor bending over him. "It is time to go," he said, while bending to retrieve the fire-blackened pot and replacing it in his pack.

Therseus stood, stretching his limbs, when he caught movement out of the corner of his eye. He turned and found himself confronted by a scaled being easily as tall as Loekor, but not as heavy. "What?" he managed to get out before his speech fled him.

Loekor looked to his young friend and spotted the creature that had startled Therseus. He slowly walked over to him, placing a large hand on his shoulder, while standing beside him. The creature returned their stare with unblinking lidless eyes. Loekor felt himself start, even as he felt Therseus jump, when the creature opened its mouth and spoke in a deep guttural voice. "What are you doing here in the swamp of Queen Larzon?" After asking this, the creature grew quiet, while extending a long forked tongue and tasting the air.

The witch stepped forward to stand in front of her two companions. "I am Cassis, the witch of the Blue Forest. I must cross this swamp on an urgent errand, and these two are my traveling companions."

The creature flicked his long scaled tail, while thinking on this information, before he spoke again. "We have heard of you, Blue Witch, and you are welcome here." Saying this, he raised his arm, as other apparitions rose up out of the muck to stand beside him. "Will you not join us, so that you may pay homage to our Queen?"

"Though we are in a great hurry," answered Cassis, "we would be honored to see your Queen, for she is an old friend of mine."

Walking in single file, they proceeded through the treacherous swamp with the scaled creatures leading the way. It was clear they disdained the hard ground they were walking on and preferred the muck that bubbled alongside the small path.

Loekor walked up beside Cassis. "Do we have time for this?" he asked while staring out over the head of his escort and seeing nothing but a dense grey fog.

"We must take the time," answered Cassis. The scaled people could be valuable allies. "Besides, the Queen is an old friend of mine, and it would not be proper to pass her lands without paying our respects," Cassis added.

Therseus stared with fascination at the strange biped creatures with the wide webbed feet and clawed hands. He was so intent on his staring that he tripped over a clump of growth and almost stumbled into the mire. He was saved from this when one of the scaled people stepped forward to grasp him, helping him regain his balance.

"I would be careful, young one," said the creature. "There are many things in this swamp that would find you very tasty." He fell back in line with his comrades after admonishing Therseus for his carelessness.

They walked half a day with the fog gradually thinning until they burst out into a small dry clearing with a small lake decorating the landscape. Looking toward its shores, Therseus noticed several small mud huts lining the bank of the lake for easy access into the water. They continued until they stood before a mud hut several times larger than the rest, with two guards standing sentry at its entrance. The guards stood at attention at the small party's approach. The sunlight gleamed brightly off the strange spears and helmets adorning their heads.

"We seek an audience with Queen Larzon. Will you not announce us?" asked Kazoon, the first reptilian creature they had spotted earlier that day. The three travelers had found out his name was Kazoon and that he was a captain in the Royal Scouts.

Entering the mud structure, Loekor and Therseus were amazed by the furnishings found in the mud dwelling. Silken tapestries lined the walls, while a rich red carpet muffled their footfalls as they made their way down a long narrow corridor leading into the central room where Queen Larzon sat upon a raised throne. She was being waited upon by several servants dressed in a green cloth fabric that accented their reddish hides.

Seeing Cassis, the Queen sprang from her throne and rushed across the room to embrace her old friend. "It has been too many years, Cassis," said Queen Larzon, while taking stock of Cassis's traveling companions.

"May I present my two friends?" asked Cassis.

"But of course," replied the Queen, staring at Therseus and making him uncomfortable with her unblinking eyes.

"This is Loekor, a brave warrior, and young Therseus, also a brave warrior from the Forest of Tearn, forest of man."

Putting her hand on the Queen's proffered arm, they proceeded to the throne while engaged in an animated conversation. Loekor glanced at Therseus and gave a barely perceptible nod of the head and a quick grin before seating himself on one of the many silk cushions scattered around the throne for that purpose.

As the feast wound down, Cassis bid farewell to Queen Larzon and they were soon off with a party of scouts to lead them through the swamp. The young female reptilians took great pleasure in flirting with Therseus, who was enjoying being the center of their attention, while Loekor conversed with the party of scouts who had led them here.

After trudging through the murky swamp for some time, the goblin couldn't help but complain. "What are we doing here?" he grumbled, swatting at a large insect. "Surely there is no one to endanger our army unless it be these blood-sucking bugs." The fat goblin leading the procession growled, "Quiet you idiot before I have you spitted."

Despite the goblin's grumbling, Loekor's keen senses detected something amiss. "There is a foul stench upon the air," he said, stopping to scent the air. "If my nose does not deceive me, I believe it is coming from the direction we are traveling to." The animals of the swamp inspected the line of goblins as they passed, sweeping their lanterns before them to dispel the darkness that was quickly closing in, cloaking them in its damp embrace.

Hearing this, two of the reptilian people slipped quietly into the bubbling muck and were soon swallowed up in its depths. The sounds of clanking armor making its way through the dense fog added to the cacophony of other noises chorused by the denizens who knew the swamp as their territory. "What was that splashing?" asked one of the goblins with fright sounding in his croaking voice.

The captain spun around to walk back among his troops. "I do not know who said that and I don't want to know," he bellowed, his raised voice echoing back at him from the fog, giving it an ethereal sound. "We belong to the army of the Dark One and we will go forth in his glory to conquer our enemies. We fear nothing!" Glaring at his troops, he continued to parade up and down the line of marchers. Satisfied, he marched back to the front of the line to resume his slow march through the swamp.

"How many?" asked Loekor after hearing the news of the goblins' approach.

"We are not sure!" answered Kazoon. The fog is very thick today." He stood in front of Loekor swishing his large tail back and forth while relaying this information. "They saw as many as you have fingers on your hands."

"What do you suggest we do, Captain?" asked Loekor, knowing they would be better off having someone in command of their small party who knew the terrain.

Pleased by the mantle of command, Kazoon fairly beamed as he laid plans for the goblins that would soon appear on the narrow path.

Loekor tensed as the line of goblins came into view. He looked to his right and saw Therseus clutching his bow until his knuckles were white. "Easy, Therseus," whispered Loekor, giving Therseus a reassuring pat on the shoulder and receiving a weak grin from the young man.

"Now!" screamed Kazoon as the marchers came abreast of them. Already there were sounds of battle and screams of agony from the rear of the column. The scouts Kazoon had sent for rear guard action were wreaking a bloody massacre on the goblins unfortunate enough to be caught unaware in the rear of the line.

There was a small twang as Therseus loosed his arrow in the direction of the lead goblin, who was

already shouting orders to restore his troops' sense of order so that they might retaliate against their attackers. The arrow caught him high in the chest, knocking the wind from him as it plowed its bloody path through him until the shaft's feathers came to rest upon his rusted breastplate. Looking down in disbelief, he snapped the end of the shaft off as he fell into the muck, which quickly embraced him in his death throes. Pandemonium was complete as Loekor and his allies fell in among the goblins, with Loekor impaling a hapless goblin on his mighty antlers, while holding two aloft in his hands until life fled their squat bodies. Kazoon could be seen using his tail as a lethal weapon, felling all who came in contact with its lashing fury.

Therseus, spending all his arrows, drew his skinning knife and leapt to his feet, but the battle was over as quickly as it had begun. The bodies of the goblins seemed to be lying everywhere, but were soon disposed of as they were unceremoniously tossed into the bubbling swamp, to the delight of the population inhabiting its depths.

Walking up to stand beside Loekor and Therseus, who were trying very hard not to let the carnage bother them, Kazoon said, "I believe you may journey safely from here." Saying this, he dipped his tail into the brackish water to erase the green-colored blood stains that had led to many a goblin's demise. "I fear it is important for me and my scouts to return to my Queen, to give warning of this trespass upon our lands."

"I can ask for no more than what you have already done, Captain," replied Loekor, grasping Kazoon's forearm in a warrior's handshake. "I shall not soon forget I have a friend and ally found here."

"I detect no more goblins," said Cassis, walking up to join the small group. "I should resent being left out of the battle, my friends."

"On the contrary, Cassis," replied Loekor, "without your friendship with Queen Larzon, it would be very possible for us to be feeding the animals and fish of this swamp."

"I suppose so," said Cassis, her feelings mollified for the moment.

With their farewells said, the two groups separated, one heading for the center of the swamp while the other warily marched onward toward the outer reaches of the vast marshes.

CHAPTER TEN

The Truce of the Dark Elves

King Illson declared a feast to honor Cassis, who was fast approaching his small kingdom. Fatted calves were slaughtered and made ready as barrels of the King's own wine were brought forth from the lower reaches of his palace. The populace was in a jubilant mood as jugglers, acrobats, and minstrels made their way to the palace so that they might ply their trade while games of skill and other contests were set up in the large courtyard of the palace.

Aeso and Maloc were well into the hills before a black-clad figure appeared before them, beckoning them to follow in his wake. Aeso swallowed and noisily cleared his throat, hesitating, then fell in behind his friend, ever watchful of the surrounding terrain, knowing he was defenseless if he were attacked. "It is the first step toward peace," he repeated over and over to himself, trying to dispel the fear that settled over his slight frame.

Turning, the Dark Elf bid them wait while he stole ahead to scout the terrain before continuing on.

Aeso, glad of this respite, sat himself on a large rock and wiped the sweat from his brow while inviting Maloc to share his resting place. "I don't mind telling you, old friend, I'm just a little afraid," said Aeso sipping from a small flask and offering the same to Maloc. "This is a journey of peace, and you will be treated accordingly. Of this I have the leader of the Dark Elves' word." No sooner had he said this than a small contingent of dark-clad figures appeared before them upsetting Aeso causing him to drop the wine flask spilling the dark red contents upon the ground.

"Do not fear, Adviser," said the largest of these elves with amusement sounding in his tone. "We are here to protect, as well as guide you to our camp, sir."

Regaining some of his lost composure, Aeso said, "For this, I thank you." Rising from his seat, he gave a small bow in the large elf's direction.

"If you are ready, sir, we may continue, for it is but a short way to our camp from here." The large elf motioned for two of the elves to proceed ahead so that they might scout ahead for possible ambushes. The Dark Elves were well aware of the consequences they would have to suffer if something happened to the King's Chief Adviser, whether it be their fault or not.

Walking through a stand of trees, they entered a meadow with a fire burning in its center. Around this sat a large number of elves in animated conversation but upon seeing the Advisor's arrival, they grew silent, some moving away from the circle to stand a short distance away talking in hushed voices as they took stock in the Chief Adviser.

"Welcome," invited the elf known as Lark standing and bowing to Aeso. "Will you not share my seat with me?"

Seating himself on the fur that had been lain upon the ground, the Chief Adviser soon found a clay mug filled with wine in his hand and raising the mug to his lips found his hand trembling uncontrollably. Tasting the wine he recognized the strange flavor and looked across the fire nodding to his friend Maloc who was in conversation with several of the black-clad figures but looked up long enough to catch Aeso's nod. Well thought Aeso to himself I would have found out sooner or later I hold no ill will toward these Elves.

"So Adviser," said Lark. "Do we talk of what brings you here?"

"Are you the leader of this...uh...band of Elves?" asked Aeso.

Lark, looking toward Maloc, found the seer staring intently at him while nodding his head. "Yes," answered Lark. "Yes, I am the leader of what you call the Dark Elves."

"Well then, by all means, let us talk of this danger that lays before us and what measures we must take to prevent it from destroying our world." The nervousness Aeso had felt earlier quickly dispelled itself as he bent to the task of uniting the Elves to fight this dark force that had thrust itself upon this world. "King Illson has granted me the power to call a truce to our petty grievances so that we might join forces to battle this dark plague."

"That is well and good," said Lark. "But I would not call the division of the Elves a petty grievance, sir. I am sure you know why this division occurred."

"Yes, well uh...we must put aside our differences even if it just be long enough to wage this war we must fight."

"Can we?" asked Lark.

"We must!" answered Aeso.

"If we ally ourselves with you what guarantees can you give us that we will be permitted to return to our homes here in the surrounding country? We are tired of being the outcasts of the Elvish Kingdom."

Aeso well understood the dilemma Lark would be putting himself in if he joined his forces with those of King Illson's. After all, these were treacherous times. He also understood the veiled threat that had been implied. "I offer myself as a hostage. I can do nothing more but give you my word and hope that will be enough." After saying this he drained the clay mug to steady his nerves without much success.

"I understand Cassis is on her way to the kingdom."

"Yes," answered Aeso. "Yes, she is."

"Then it may be possible," Lark said. "There is not an elf here that would not stand behind Cassis in a fight." Putting his fingers to his mouth, he whistled, and soon the clearing was filled to capacity as hundreds of elves came out of hiding. "I hope you will forgive, sir. It could have been a trap."

"I can see you would be a valuable ally," said Aeso as he took stock in the number of elves that had hidden in case it had been a trap.

Lark could not help laughing at the expression on Aeso's face. "It may be so, Adviser. It may be so," he said, slapping Aeso on the back in a not unfriendly gesture. "Bring more wine so that we may drink to this truce. We rest tonight, for on the morrow we journey to the court of King Illson."

Miles away as the meeting between Lark and the Chief Adviser was taking place, three shapes sat huddled around a small campfire talking in low tones so as not to arouse unwanted visitors.

"I hope we find our arrival welcoming," said Loekor, adding a few sticks to the fire while keeping a watchful eye on the darkness surrounding them.

"Do not fear," said Cassis as she wrapped her blue cloak around herself. "I am sure you will find we are more than welcome."

"What are the elves like?" asked Therseus, letting his boyish curiosity get the best of him.

"They are a proud race," answered Cassis then thinking added, "At least that is the way it was when I last saw them. You will find them not unlike yourself in appearance my young friend."

"Oh," said Therseus feeling a little disappointed at what he thought to be a mystic people.

"But," said Cassis letting the word hang in the air and finding amusement in Therseus' renewed attention. "They are different from you in a lot of other ways though."

"What other ways?" asked Therseus leaning closer to Cassis.

Chuckling Cassis answered, "You will see on the morrow for we shall be there then."

CHAPTER ELEVEN
Arrival at the Palace

The small furred animals took flight after scolding the line of marchers in high-pitched, squeaking voices. Soon the air was filled with the small creatures, all emitting high-pitched sounds that deafened the Dark Elves' footfalls as they steadily marched towards the Elf Kingdom that lay directly ahead. It was a quiet line of marchers, each Elf lost in his own thoughts, some doubting the wisdom of this venture but willing to follow their leader no matter what might befall them. After another hour of marching, they halted in a stand of yellow-barked trees and waited for the return of the scouts who had been sent ahead. Many partook of the fleshy leaves, enjoying the sweetish taste, not unlike sugarcane and gold in color. In a short while, two of the scouts returned to report their findings.

"It seems they are preparing a feast, Captain," said the first of the scouts to reach the stand of trees.

"Mayhap that is a good omen," said Lark, as a thoughtful expression crossed his face.

Aeso and Maloc came to stand beside Lark, curious to find out what the scout had reported.

"It seems, Adviser, of what you say, must be true." Lark continued to survey their immediate surroundings with a practiced eye. "A vast army could still be hidden within that city, though."

"Believe me when I say you are welcome inside the kingdom this day," Aeso said, wondering what Lark would do if he knew the real condition of the king's army and of the pitiful number that still wore the king's colors. Lark's Dark Elves could easily overwhelm the king's army without much of a fight, given the arms. Maloc gave Aeso a knowing look, as if he knew Aeso's thought on this, making him uncomfortable.

"Twenty elves by me," said Lark. "The rest wait here until I send for you. If word has not reached you on the hour, a trap has been sprung."

Approaching the gates leading into the kingdom, two sentries stood at rigid attention, although it was plain to see they were more than a little surprised to see the Chief Adviser leading the small party of Dark Elves. A group of gaily dressed elves, slightly drunk, staggered over to gawk at the new arrivals within the city walls. Soon they were talking in hushed tones among themselves as they followed the Dark Elves toward the palace. "That is Captain Lark, is it not?" asked one of the revelers.

"Yes," answered another. "Yes, that is him."

Soon they entered the courtyard of the palace, causing a quietness to settle over the large crowd gathered there. As the new arrivals approached, the elves parted before them while trying to get a better look at what they called the Dark Elves. Passing into the palace, the crowd resumed their merry-making while stealing glances towards the palace and murmuring amongst themselves. Finally, they arrived at a small rise overlooking a large valley. 'Is that the Kingdom of the Elves?' asked Therseus, standing atop the rise and gazing down at the drab buildings and tall walls surrounding them. 'Yes,' answered Cassis, her eyes wandering over the landscape. 'It is not what I expected,' said Therseus. 'Nor I, young friend. Things must have changed much with the passing of time. Still, do not let your eyes deceive you."

Shouldering his pack, Loekor started ahead of his two companions, acutely aware of being watched but deciding not to mention it in front of Therseus, for he guessed Cassis already knew.

Trudging down the small hillock, they were soon within yelling distance of the gate leading into the kingdom and were challenged by a disembodied voice. "Who might you be, strangers?"

Cassis, pushing her way past Loekor, replied, "It is I, Cassis, of the Blue Forest, with two friends of your kingdom." Saying this, she added, "Is this how you treat friends of your kingdom?"

They could hear the murmur of voices before discerning a heavy latch being lifted, then the gates swung open, emitting a platoon of soldiers dressed in their best uniforms, some carrying pikes while others nervously fingered the swords hanging by their sides.

"Colorful," thought Loekor, admiring the smooth green leather of their tunics while not missing the thigh-high boots, purple in color. Getting closer, Loekor figured they could not be more than four feet tall, but by the set faces, he guessed they would be a force to be reckoned with.

Intent upon the elves' approach, Loekor and Therseus did not notice the blue cloud enveloping Cassis until the elves drew even closer, till at last, they halted not twenty feet away, with mouths agape.

"What the—" Loekor managed to say before the blue cloud drifted to put itself between himself and the soldiers, who were nervously starting to mill about.

A voice sounded from within the cloud, "Is there doubt to who I am now?"

Bowing, the foremost elf replied, "Please forgive me, Cassis, but I have my orders. These are uneasy times. If I may present myself?"

"You may."

"I am Iston, Captain of the wall guard. If you would follow me, it would be my honor to escort you and your friends to the palace." He fell silent, waiting for a reply.

"I and my companions would be honored, Captain Iston," answered Cassis, resuming her former shape.

It took the whole platoon to break a path through the curious elves, who wanted a closer look at these strange beings, especially Loekor and Therseus, who were giants among them. Every once in a while, a voice could be heard within the large crowd, threatening to engulf them. "Cassis, do you remember me?"

She made it a point to nod in the direction from whence the voice would come, although she could not discern a familiar face in the throng of elves, being there were so many.

"I hope you will forgive these elves, Cassis," said Captain Iston. "But with your two friends, I'm afraid you do present a spectacle worth seeing."

"It is no bother, Captain," replied Cassis, glancing at her two traveling companions who, at the moment, were gazing around in wonder themselves.

Therseus, bedazzled at the multitude of elves, said to Loekor, "I have never seen so many people in one place."

Thinking, he corrected himself, "I meant elves."

Loekor bent down so that he could reply, the voices of the elves making it almost impossible to talk. "I know what you mean, young friend."

Arriving at the palace's large courtyard, a scene of gaiety and feasting unfolded before them, with strange aromas coming from large pits as elves dressed in somber blue turned the large spits with several kinds of roasting meats skewered on large poles.

Therseus unconsciously licked his lips, passing by these before stopping to converse with one of the cooks and was rewarded with a large piece of meat he could not identify but found it very tasty. Further on, they passed large tables overburdened with fruits, cheese, and a large variety of breads.

"Would you like refreshment?" asked an elf dressed in reddish velvet, tending huge wooden drums of wine.

"I would like it very much," replied Loekor. "But first, we must present ourselves to your King."

Passing through the courtyard amid the curious stares of the gaily dressed populace, loud voices could be heard coming from the palace's interior.

"This is where I leave you," spoke Captain Iston, bowing and returning to the walls with his platoon.

Loekor and Therseus glanced at each other, each wondering if they should venture further when Cassis turned, saying, "Come, we must present ourselves before the King." They proceeded through the dimly lit corridors, paying scant attention to the guards stationed there but, in return, getting wide-eyed stares from the guards. Approaching a large ornate door, they stopped before two elves dressed in maroon robes, giving each other nervous looks. Before they could speak, Cassis said, "I wish an audience with your King. Will you announce us?"

"And whom shall we say is here?" asked one of the elves, finding his tongue and pompous attitude at the same time.

"Never mind," said Cassis, raising an arm and causing the large double door to open on its own volition.

The two elves exclaimed, "Cassis!" in one voice.

Striding into the large room, Cassis approached the throne on which a figure dressed in purple silk with an amber crown encrusted with jewels was glaring at an elf dressed entirely in black before him, while another dressed in yellow held his hands out pleadingly, as if to cool the tempers of the two elves confronting each other.

The hundred or so elves whose attention was focused on the throne were caught unaware by Cassis and her two companions' approach. The King, surprised by the unexpected arrival of Cassis and her companions, jolted in his throne and nearly lost his balance, causing Lark to turn around and see what had caused the commotion. He then saw Cassis standing tall while Lark knelt on one knee, a smile creasing his face.

"Arise, Captain Lark," said Cassis. "A warrior and friend such as you has no reason to kneel before me."

"Who is this?" asked King Illson, still standing and pointing in the direction of Cassis and her two companions.

"It is Cassis, Sire," answered Aeso. "But of the other two, I know not."

Loekor picked this time to step forward, pulling Therseus along with him until they both stood before King Illson. "If I may," said Loekor, resting a steady gaze on the King, who now fidgeted on his throne, but soon recovering himself, nodded to the pair. "I am Loekor, from the Forest of Pandasia; and this young warrior is Therseus, from the Forest of Man." Saying this, he gave a slight bow, his eyes never wavering from the King's.

Therseus's knees almost buckled as he looked around the large, ornate throne room and realized that he and Loekor were the focus of the hundred pairs of eyes fixed upon them.

"You are welcome here," said King Illson. "We hope you will enjoy our festivities." He now looked at Cassis. "And you, Cassis, I have heard much. We have waited anxiously for your coming." Chuckling, he looked toward Lark and said, "I suppose that is one of the few things Lark and myself agree on." Cocking his head to one side, he listened to his Chief Adviser, Aeso, and nodded in agreement. "That is a very good idea, Aeso. Cassis, will you and your party join myself and Aeso in my apartments? And of course, we must not forget Lark.

He adds color to my drab existence." Rising from his throne, he walked through a door leading into his room, but not before dismissing the elves of his court.

Aeso beckoned for them to follow, then led the small group through a brightly lit hallway with several tapestries sharing the walls with candle holders. The air was filled with a sweetish odor, coming from the candles of various shades and hues as they burned brightly in their holders.

Therseus, looking down, noticed a soft light coming from the deep blue carpet muffling their footfalls as they continued down the seemingly endless hallway. At last, they entered a high dome-like structure where the sun streamed through the transparent ceiling, casting warm light on several strange-looking plants in a variety of colors. Walking by a large leafed plant with a rainbow of colors, Therseus stopped to inspect the multicolored leaves and jumped when it made a cooing sound. Reaching out to stroke the leaves as his curiosity got the better of him, he was rewarded with a purr. Looking up from his fascination, he noticed the party he was with disappearing through another door, and he reluctantly hurried to catch up. Walking through the door, his eyes grew wide at the room's rich furnishings. Seeing his friends seated on silken-like cushions, he walked over and seated himself; he rubbed his hand across the cushion's smooth surface, enjoying the way it felt to his touch.

The King entered through a curtained doorway, wearing a plain brown robe. Sighing, he seated himself by Aeso, across from his guests, while studying them intently. "This is much better," said King Illson. "Now, where shall we begin?"

"I suggest we find out what information Cassis and Lark have for us, Sire, and then add it to what we have learned ourselves," said Aeso, looking earnestly toward Lark and Cassis. "Are we in agreement?"

"By all means, Aeso," answered Cassis. "It would be wise to exchange information."

"If Cassis is so inclined, then so am I," said Lark. "My scouts are even now trailing a large party of goblins with human captives, but as yet, I'm still waiting for further reports on their destination, even though I am sure we all know what that destination will be."

"Then, that is where I must go," cried Therseus, jumping to his feet and finding a strong hand upon his arm. Trembling, he looked down into Loekor's eyes, finding an understanding in them that words could not convey.

Speaking softly, Loekor said, "Be patient, young warrior. Your time will come soon enough."

"The goblins are on the move again," interrupted Cassis. "For we have already given battle in Queen Kazoon's swamp. With what Lark says, we must make haste, for we are not prepared to wage a long war. If possible, we must attack the Dark One before he can achieve the Scepter of Soren, but I suggest first we free the human captives and arm them. Our numbers are pitifully small compared to the goblins, and we will need all the warriors we can gather."

A small cough caused the group to turn around, and doing so, they saw Maloc approaching with a worried frown evident upon his face. "I hope you will forgive my interruption, but I have news of great importance for this meeting."

Aeso rose, escorting his friend to the small group. "Sire, may I present Maloc, the Seer, a wise and just elf?"

"But of course," answered King Illson, gesturing for them to be seated. "What of this news you have for us, Seer?"

"A large army of goblins, even as we speak, marches to the Kingdom of the Elves, here," said Maloc. Taking a breath, he continued, "I fear they will be here within the week, if not stopped."

"Then, there is no time to waste," said Lark. "I will send two hundred elves to free the humans, although it is not in my power to arm them."

"That presents no problem," said Aeso, looking toward the King and receiving a nod to continue. "We have a large store of weapons."

Therseus said, "I wish to go," feeling his blood grow hot at the idea of his people being enslaved.

"If that is what you wish, young warrior," said Lark. "But you remember that you will have to follow orders as if you were one of my elves."

"I thank you," replied Therseus, growing quiet while brooding on the plight of his people.

Cassis interrupted all other conversations, her voice sharp with anger. 'In my visions, I saw the elves splitting their forces,' she said, glaring at King Illson. 'This was a source of great sadness for me, but I believe that the elves have realized their mistake. Now, more than ever, it is important to put aside our differences and work together. The split among the elves has eroded trust and weakened our defenses. We must work together and rebuild that trust if we hope to prevail in this war.

With this said, Lark rose, extending his hand toward King Illson, who clasped it in a warrior's handshake. "I, leader of the Dark Elves, acknowledge you as King... For now. We are at your bidding, Sire."

"Now," said Cassis, satisfied. "First, we will free the humans. As you already know, Loekor, you are the chosen one to free the Scepter of Soren. I should have told you sooner, but I needed to confirm my visions and be certain that it was you I had been waiting for."

"But how?" stammered Loekor.

"You will find a way," replied Cassis. "It is ordained. With Maloc's help, I will attempt to spy on the Dark One so we might better know his plans. Thirdly, King Illson and Lark will lead an army to meet the goblins that approach. Is everyone agreed?"

There was a nod of heads, each lost in their own thoughts.

"Today is a day of feasting," said Cassis. "Lark, call your elves, for on the morrow we begin."

"And what of my kingdom?" asked King Illson. "What will my subjects think if I abandon the city?"

"You can spare enough elves to protect your city, but for now, what is important, is for your subjects to see that you and Lark are united in one common cause. It will give them hope, your subjects, as well as Lark's Dark Elves."

The meeting over, the plans laid, the solemn group filed out, leaving King Illson and Aeso to ponder over the current change of events.

"Do you think it wise to place ourselves in Cassis' hands?" asked King Illson.

"Her plans sound wise. Besides, with her here, we can expect no trouble from the Dark Elves, for they have a great respect for her, as well as I myself have. I think we have cut ourselves off from the rest of this world for far too long. With her help, and of course Lark's, I believe we can recoup the glory that was once ours. Do you not wonder at times what the rest of this world is like, and the beings we share it with?"

"Yes, Aeso. I have often wondered what lies beyond this kingdom's walls. As you know, I have very seldom left this sanctuary I call a palace for fear of reprisals from the Dark Elves, but meeting Lark, I find my fears unfounded."

"Then mayhap the Dark Lord can benefit the Elves. If," he muttered, "he does not destroy us."

"Aeso, let us go forth so that we might feast with our subjects, as well as our new friends. It has been long since the elves have seen their King," said King Illson.

CHAPTER TWELVE
The Goblin Proposal

"The King," someone shouted, causing all to turn and stare, then bow to the figure approaching them from the palace.

"Arise," shouted King Illson, "so that all might hear. Let it be known that on this day, that all Elves know as the Dark Elves shall be treated as friends and brothers."

Decreeing this, he continued: "It has been too long since we have ventured from this place we call home." He had to quiet the crowd, roaring its approval, before saying anything else. "I only hope it is not too late, for on the morrow I march to meet a threat — a threat that could destroy our future. I call on all elves to join me — to meet this threat. So we may conquer this enemy, who even now plots to destroy us."

All grew quiet, digesting this news, when suddenly, the air was filled with someone shouting. "Long live King Illson," which grew like a tidal wave as thousands of elves repeated it, soon growing to a roaring chant, drowning out all other noise. A black-clad figure fought his way through the crowd and upon reaching the King, grabbed his hand, raising it for all to see, and shouted: "Long live King Illson."

"That is Lark, is it not?"

"Yes," answered another. "That is indeed, Lark."

The large multitude of elves, their eyes fastened on their King and Lark, paid scant attention to the company of black-clad elves dragging a spitting and kicking figure (purple in color), wearing an enormous mail shirt before them as they pushed their way through the throng of elves, intent upon reaching Lark and King Illson.

Lark, noticing this from his vantage point, directed the King's gaze in the direction of the elves' approach with a prisoner, and a vile looking one at that.

The goblin, finding himself in front of the two elves, guessed this to be their leaders, and snarled from a mouth resembling a small cave, "Is this how you treat an ambassador of peace?"

"No, it is not!" answered King Illson. "However, it is how we treat a thousand-year-old enemy."

The large crowd of elves had grown so quiet over this exchange that, if perchance a pin had been dropped, it would have sounded like a gong. A chant started and continued until it had become a roar almost unbearable to the ear.

"Long live the elves!"

King Illson raised his arm, quieting the elves once more. "We will hear him out. For be it not said, the elves are not honorable warriors." Turning, he walked back to the palace with Lark close on his heels, followed by the Dark Elves dragging the screaming, cursing goblin with them.

Entering the audience chamber, King Illson was mildly surprised to find Cassis and her two companions waiting for him, as well as Aeso and Maloc. Seating himself once again on the throne, he commanded the prisoner to be brought before him.

The Dark Elves glanced toward Lark, who gave a slight nod, much to the King's irritation.

It was at this time Aeso placed himself at the King's side, murmuring, "Remember, my King, Lark has been their leader these hundreds of years."

"Yes, yes, I see your point," answered the King, still irritated but trying very hard not to show it as he nibbled on his bottom lip.

The Dark Elves approached the throne, and upon bowing, threw their prisoner before them so that he lay prostrate before the King.

The goblin, cursing and growling, had difficulty raising himself up, for it was clear the mail shirt was heavy and meant for a creature far larger than the squat goblin.

Loekor stepped forward, grasping the mail shirt by the collar, jerking the goblin up quite easily, setting the foul creature back upon his overly large feet.

At a nod and a slight grin from the King, who was having difficulty keeping the amusement from showing upon his countenance, Loekor bowed, stepping back to join Cassis and Therseus.

Therseus, taking stock in the proceeding, stared at the creature, fascinated by the purple skin battling the warts for control of the small compact body. He had not had the chance to study the creatures they had battled in the swamps of Queen Larzon, for the bodies had been disposed of very quickly.

"May I ask what brings you before the mighty King Illson?" asked Aeso in a commanding voice.

The goblin sneeringly replied, "My fearless and brave leader, Grildon, has sent me to ask your help in overthrowing the Dark Lord."

Astonishment was plainly registered on every face, the only sound being the goblin's own harsh breathing.

"Choose your words well," whispered Aeso in the King's ear. "Mayhap it can be a great boon."

"And where is your leader to be found?" asked King Illson, nonchalance sounding in his voice.

The goblin, staring balefully, answered, "he is even now crossing the Plains of Leon with a large and powerful army."

Cassis placed a hand on the goblin's shoulder, causing him to jump and almost topple over. Turning and finding himself confronted by Cassis, he snarled, "Get away from me, old woman."

Lark said, "I would watch my mouth, foul one. Do you not know Cassis, witch of the Blue Forest?"

A startled yelp issued from the goblin's mouth as he toppled over in his hurry to get away from Cassis.

"Do not fear, my ugly one," said Cassis, raising a hand, causing the startled goblin to float gently from the floor until at last, he was back on his feet. "What he says is true, of this I am sure, but the reason for this evades me."

"The reason is simple," croaked the goblin. "My leader does not wish to go to war. Although our lands are poor, and our lives simple, we cherish these. Besides, Kowlock — I mean the Dark Lord offers nothing for our services. Why should we throw our lives away for nothing, when nothing is something we have more than enough of already?"

"If your leader does not wish to go to war, why is it he wishes to ally himself with the elves, who will surely defend what is theirs? Be it their lives, homes or freedom," asked King Illson.

The goblin, squinting his large saucer-like eyes, replied, "I did not say our services would be free, but before you ask anything else, remember, our lives are a simple one, as well as our needs."

"And what fees are we speaking of?" asked King Illson, his brow furrowed in contemplation.

"We would require the lands east of here for a thousand square miles... Also, as much wine as five hundred goblins might carry."

"Is this all?" asked the King.

"No, we would also like the elves' word that they would ally themselves with us if future trouble arose...and..."

"Go on."

"We would like you to arm our army with your fine elvish weapons." Asking this, he rocked back and forth until he was almost sitting on the floor, while staring balefully at those closest to him.

"Take our guest out so that he might enjoy the fine wines and foods of our festivities," said the King. "We must talk of this in private before we give our answer."

Turning, the goblin walked toward the courtyard with the dark-clad elves walking on either side of him, not so much as to keep the goblin from escaping but to keep him safe from the elves outside who would surely do him harm. A thousand-year-old enemy is not one to be forgiven so easily.

"Well," the king said to no one in particular, "this does present a new problem, does it not?"

"Not so," said Lark. "It would be most easy to dispatch this foul-mouthed creature, being they are treacherous and not to be trusted. I would be more than happy to show this goblin the same courtesy they bestowed on the elves in the last Goblin Wars. It is fair and just."

The King said, "I am inclined to agree with you, but still..."

"Do not be hasty on this decision," said Cassis. "It is true that goblins are a most treacherous lot and would gladly align themselves with the winning side, be it us or the Dark One. So it is very clear for now, they figure we are a force to be reckoned with. It might be wise to take advantage of this, for as soon as the other goblins hear of this, it stands to reason the other goblins could be swayed to fight on our side, even if it be just till we defeat the Dark One and his minions. Without his leadership, the goblins would be of no threat; and we must not overlook the possibility that they give their word in all sincerity. Although this is doubtful. We could divide the goblin army on some pretense, and if indeed it is treachery on the Dark One's part. The goblins could be defeated more easily, and without much loss of life. I would be the first to say it is a gamble, but a gamble well worth taking. The final decision rests with you, King Illson. Your word will be accepted and obeyed."

All eyes turned to the young King, who rested his chin on a clenched fist while pondering the problem of what to do about the goblins, his face showing indecision. "Would anyone else speak?" he asked.

"Yes," answered Lark. "Yes, I would like to speak."

Approaching the throne, he clenched his hands at his sides while a dark scowl played upon his face. "If you had been there in the goblin wars, Sire, you would know quite well why I say kill the goblin and destroy his wretched army." Looking beseechingly at the King, he continued, "It is the only way. They are a sorry lot and would destroy us if chance prevailed."

"Mayhap you are right, Lark," sighed the King. "But you must agree, they could be an invaluable ally in this dark time."

"Yes, Sire, I will admit that," said Lark, bowing his head and trudging back to once more stand beside Cassis.

The King, looking toward the small group, sighed and said, "Let me ponder over these arguments. I will send a guard to fetch you back when I have reached my decision, which will surely be soon, and Cassis, if you would remain..."

"Yes, King Illson," answered Cassis, hearing retreating footsteps and then a large door closing quietly.

Upon reaching the courtyard, Lark made his way to a band of his elves, who at this time were drinking wine while waiting for their leader, and seeing the scowl on his face, grew quiet at his approach.

Loekor and Therseus, watching the retreating back, shrugged and made their way to a table laden with a large variety of meats, and sating their hunger, strolled through the streets, taking in the sights while carrying on a hushed conversation.

"I must go and help my people," said Therseus, his voice charged with emotion. "But I must tell you, Loekor, I will sorely miss your company once we part ways."

"I know, young friend. I know," replied Loekor, pausing to admire the intricate carvings found on the doors leading into the elves' houses. Each door told a different story. "I have grown quite fond of you, and I could not ask for a better warrior to guard my back." Pausing, he placed a hand on Therseus's shoulder. "But it seems that from here, we must tread our different paths and hope they will cross again." Taking a deep breath, he continued, "When this is over, mayhap we might explore this world before returning to our homelands."

"I would like that," replied Therseus, a tear traveling unnoticed down his cheek.

Before reaching the palace's courtyard, Therseus asked, "Do you think Lark is right in what he says?"

"Yes," answered Loekor, "but I also believe what Cassis said to be true. We will wait for King Illson's decision, for it is in his hands now."

"Are you not a king yourself? Does this not give you a right to have your say?"

"In my homeland, I am a king, but here, I am just a stranger, much like yourself. But then, a king in my homeland is just a title and nothing more, my young friend," explained Loekor, seeing Therseus perplexed. "My father's father decided a long time ago it was better to have a council to settle matters, instead of one horned one. In this way, all arguments are heard and settled upon. Even though I have to sit in council, it still leaves me time to explore, hunt, fish, or do whatever it is I wish to do. I find this very agreeable and would not change it."

"Almost like my own village," said Therseus.

Entering the courtyard, they spent their time sampling the wine and fruits while engaging different elves in conversation. Being an oddity, they attracted a large number of elves who wanted a closer look at these two strangers and information about their homelands.

Leaving Loekor in the midst of the inquiring elves, Therseus made his way to Lark, who was still wearing a scowl on his face and gesturing angrily while confronting an elf a foot taller than himself and sporting a head full of unruly red hair.

"But why must we--"

"Enough!" said Lark, noticing Therseus approach.

Lark gave Therseus a beaming smile and a slight bow as he reached the tight-knit group of elves. "Welcome, young warrior. May I present Grimdom. It is he who will lead the party that will free your fellow humans."

Therseus bowed to Grimdom and said, "I hope you will find me a worthy warrior on the morrow, sir."

Impressed with the courtesy, Grimdom said, "I am sure you will do your part, young one."

As the elves grew quiet, Therseus felt a growing sense of unease and turned to leave. Before he could take a step, however, a firm hand was laid on his shoulder, holding him in place. He turned to see Lark standing beside him, his expression serious. "Please stay," said Lark. "I would like your opinion on the matter of the goblins."

"Sir, I am just a stranger in your lands, and I am sure my opinion is of little importance," said Therseus. With the elves staring at him, he felt as if a hand had been placed at his throat. "But if you insist..." The elves continued staring with unwavering eyes.

"Therseus," Loekor said, approaching the tense group.

"We are waiting for this young man's opinion," said Lark, annoyed at the interruption.

Loekor replied, "Do you not think he is young and inexperienced for what you ask?"

"Mayhap you are right, but how about you?"

"I will wait for the King's answer," said Loekor, steering Therseus away from the sullen group.

The elves stared at the retreating back, but soon forgot them as they disappeared into the crowd. However, before the two could explore further, they were summoned back to the palace.

Upon arrival, they saw Lark already there, with a look of triumph adorning his face. Their eyes searched but could not see any goblin evidence.

The King, satisfied that everyone was present, proceeded, "It has been decided. We have sent the goblin back to report to his commander that all is well. But I must agree with Lark that the goblins are a treacherous race, and so being, Lark will take part of his forces to come from behind, and I, myself, will lead my army to confront this commander. If it is a trap, we will have them in the middle. If it is not a trap, I will gladly fight at their side, but they shall not be armed with elvish weapons."

"What of my people?" cried Therseus.

Holding his hand up for silence, the King continued, "Grimdom, as Lark tells me, will lead a part of his forces to free the human captives and lead them back here to arm the men and hold the women safe. Cassis has informed me that she will proceed with Loekor to Mount Kan to try to recover the scepter. Now, my friends, it is almost time for us to go our separate ways."

Clapping his hands, servants appeared bearing trays with goblets of wine. The King raised his goblet and said, "My friends, to us, to our quest, and to the Dark One's demise."

CHAPTER THIRTEEN
Plains of Peril

With the coming of morning, Therseus awoke to the reddish sunbeams playing tag upon his face, and turning over, he noticed the bed that had contained Loekor last night was empty. He hurriedly dressed and ran out into the courtyard, almost ramming into the King's mount, which shied from his advance.

While staring at the six-legged beast, he asked, "Have you seen Loekor, Sire?" "Cassis woke him earlier saying they must hurry to Mount Kan." The King had his hands full trying to control the scaled beast, which was now squealing and trying to bite Therseus. "Perhaps it had something to do with what she saw with Maloc last night. They left in such a hurry I, myself, did not have the opportunity to talk with them, and as for Maloc, he left with them. If you will excuse me, my beast seems to have taken a disliking to you."

As Therseus watched, a horn sprouted from the creature's head, but before he could ask what this strange perturbation was, Lark made an appearance and ushered the young man away. Catching Therseus by the arm, Lark steered him towards a tent that had been set up earlier.

"Dress? But I am dressed," said Therseus while looking down upon himself. "I believe Grimdom has something a little more fitting for a warrior of the Dark Elves."

Lark led him through the tent's entrance, and inside they found Grimdom impatiently waiting within.

"This is for you, young one, and I hope it fits," said Grimdom, handing him a shirt and britches made from a dark material.

"For me?" stammered Therseus, feeling the soft satiny fabric. "Yes," answered Grimdom, tapping his foot to better emphasize his impatience. "Thank you, sir," said Therseus, donning the black shirt and britches and feeling as though he wore nothing at all. "It's a perfect fit, and a wonderful present." "It is nothing." Grimdom, try as he might, could not hide the grin that lit up his own face. "Let's not forget this," he said, handing Therseus a mailed shirt so sheer and light, a spider might have woven it.

"Therseus," Lark called from across the tent, and turning, he found a bone-white bow being pitched to him along with a quiver of arrows made from the same material.

Studying the bow, Therseus could not decide if it were metal or wood, but was delighted to find it weighed but a few ounces and was amazed to find it very hard to pull the string back. "A most wondrous bow, sir. How am I to thank you?" "Shoot straight, young warrior," answered Lark, striding over and buckling a wide black belt on Therseus, then sliding a short ornate sword into its scabbard.

Grimdom and Lark stood back to better appraise the young man before them. "What do you think?" asked Lark. "Rather large for an elf, but I think he'll do," answered Grimdom, the grin on his face growing wider.

"Excuse me, but might you tell me what sort of strange beast the King is mounted on?" "It is a Norn," replied Lark. "Keep your distance, for if it doesn't trample you, its bite is venomous as well as its horn." "I will heed your advice," said Therseus, silently grateful the King could control the beast.

"Now to see the King," said Lark, making his way toward the King with Grimdom and Therseus. Therseus strutted through the staring elves, proud of his new uniform.

The King, seeing the three approach, lifted his helm. "Ho, I see that you have made an elf out of our young warrior. You can count yourself lucky, Therseus, for no mortal has yet worn the uniform of the Elves, be it dark or my own. It is an honor, is it not, Lark?" "It is for his own protection, Sire," answered Lark. "The reason we are here is to inform you that Grimdom is ready to take his leave."

The King, stepping down from his mount, placed his hands on Therseus and Grimdom. "I wish you luck upon your quest, and hope we will meet again, so we might toast our victory."

With this said, Therseus set out with Grimdom and two hundred dour-faced elves, dressed as he was, dressed for war.

As Therseus continued along with the black wave spreading across the land, he looked back over his shoulder once more and shielded his eyes from the glare caused by the sun winking off the bone-white armor of the King's army. Meanwhile, Loekor, having placed a hand on the jutting rock, turned to see how Cassis and Maloc fared. It was then that he noticed a long line of white snaking its way across the valley floor far below.

"Wait, what is that?" Loekor asked, squinting his eyes to get a better look. Reaching down, he pulled Cassis and then Maloc up until all three stood on the precarious ledge.

Maloc, squinting against the sun's bright glare, said, "It is the King's army, and look there." His foot slipping caused a small avalanche to echo down the face of the cliff, to mingle with his surprised yelp.

Loekor, seeing the Seer's predicament, reached out, grabbing the Seer, helping him to regain his footing. With Maloc regaining a better perch, Loekor released him, while staring in the opposite direction of the King's army, and saw a fan of black-clad marchers slowly disappearing over a hill soon lost to sight. Loekor, straining his eyes, searched for Therseus, but found it impossible at this distance. "Luck be with you," he thought, turning to navigate the sheer cliff stretching above them. Not knowing Therseus was already well on his way, as he had left earlier with Grimdom.

Finally gaining the top they had sought since the early morning hours, Maloc dusted himself off while seeing that his two companions were none the worse for wear. Catching his breath, he was going to comment on this when a loud screeching filled the air, and he found himself violently flung to the ground. His breath whooshed out from him as bright pinpoints of light danced before his watering eyes.

"Do not move," Loekor hissed, approaching the squawking bird-like creature who, at the moment, was trying to get a purchase on Maloc with razor-sharp talons. He was not sure what he faced, but Loekor knew if he could distract the winged apparition for a moment, he could save Maloc from certain death.

Hearing Loekor's voice, Maloc lay as if death had already

visited him with its cold embrace. He was not sure it had not in the form of this foul creature who stood over him, flexing the razored talons while keeping an eye on the two-legged beings who warily circled him, looking for an opening.

"Loekor," whispered Cassis, pitching him a large rock and a limb from a nearby bush that started to change in shape even as his hands closed over them.

A tingling tickled his hands, and chancing a glance in her direction, he was amazed at the soft glow emanating from his clenched fists. Almost dropping the objects, he stole a look at Cassis with a questioning expression on his face.

"Trust me," said Cassis, as she made a circling motion with her hands and chanted, causing the air to shimmer and dance before her.

Loekor held his arms up and beheld a shield and sword, with smoky vapors dancing in their depths. Seeing the opening he had been waiting for, he launched himself in the direction of the scaled bird, surprising it with a furious attack. Caught off guard, the bird forgot the struggling elf beneath him as he watched his blue-black blood pump in a steady stream from the severed wing that lay twitching on the ground.

An eerie screaming filled the air as the scaled bird backed away from its intended victims. Loekor, seeing his chance, flung the shield at the bird, letting the creature's own backward momentum carry it over the cliff to fall squawking to its death far below.

"How can I thank you?" sputtered Maloc, regaining his feet and breath, still trembling uncontrollably from his near-death experience.

"I think your gratitude should go to Cassis, for without her..." Looking at his hand in bewilderment, he noticed he again held a limb from a small bush.

"In that case, my gratitude and undying loyalty goes to you both." Bowing, he then turned to the problem of wiping off the dirt from his bruised face.

Satisfied there were no serious injuries, they stared across the grassy plains before them, dotted here and there with trees much resembling a half-closed umbrella, bearing an enormous orange fruit, of which several large furred, bipedal animals fed on, some of the animals as tall as the trees, which were easily fifteen feet in height.

As they got closer, they noticed the animals bear-like in

appearance, although instead of paws ending with claws, they had hands much like humans in appearance. With these, they delicately picked the fruit. Watching them eat, they also noticed that instead of a snout bristling with teeth, these animals had a small slit of a mouth, which they fed small bits of the fruit into, while warily keeping an eye on the approach of the three travelers.

Seeing the travelers growing closer, the beasts lumbered off into the distance to feed off another tree, while still keeping a close watch.

"What strange manner of animals may these be?" asked Loekor, awed by their size, he was relieved to found out they were not meat-eaters.

"Those are Loneeks," Cassis said, gesturing towards the towering creatures. "They're gentle giants, harmlessly grazing on the fruit of those trees. They only attack if provoked, usually to protect their young. But we should keep our distance, just in case."

Reaching the tree the Loneeks had previously been grazing on, Cassis called a halt after noticing the strain that showed on Maloc's face, traveling these many miles.

"Loekor, if you will gather some of the fruit from this tree, I am sure you will find it very tasty, and a hearty meal of which, I hope you will share with Maloc and myself." Saying this, she sat under the tree, letting a sigh escape as she leaned against the cool bark of the tree, soon dozing.

She soon found herself joined by a grateful Maloc, sitting beside her, while wiping the sweat and grime wearily from his travel-stained face.

"Would you care for water?" asked Maloc, waking Cassis from her brief slumber.

Cassis shook her head and stared up into the tree's branches, watching Loekor gather the fruit, while trying to keep his precarious balance on cloven hooves, never meant to climb trees.

Loekor, satisfied he had enough, inched his way downward till at last, he stood on the ground holding tightly to his prize.

"It is not enough," said Cassis.

"It is more than so," retorted Loekor, setting the fruit down, while examining the minor scratches he had received while gathering the fruit.

"I forgot to tell you that this particular fruit will keep for a long while, and it will make good eating for our journey." So saying, she raised her arms, causing a shower of the fruit to rain down on them.

"Why did you have me climb that tree?" asked Loekor, stamping his hooves in irritation.

"It was more entertaining," answered Cassis, picking up a pear-shaped fruit, enjoying the sweet juice as she bit into its soft flesh.

"Why you—" Loekor noticed the merriment crinkling the corners of Cassis' eyes and the sly wink he received from Maloc. He shrugged, chuckling as he sat down and joined in the feast. "Forgive me, Loekor, but it does help relieve a tedious journey."

"Yes, yes, I suppose it does," agreed Loekor.

After an hour's rest, they started across the broad expanse of the plain, the grass sometimes restricting their view, as it waved in the breeze found high above their heads. Trudging through the stifling heat found below, they swatted at insects attracted by their body heat, intent upon tasting their blood, biting on their bare skin in hopes of an easy meal.

"I don't think I can go much further," gasped Maloc, looking at his arm, he felt a stinging sensation and saw a large gray insect staring back at him through large bulbous eyes as it drilled into his arm a second time. "Why you—" he uttered, bringing his hand down, squashing the insect, mingling it with his own small drops of blood.

"Just another hour or so, Maloc," said Cassis. "Then we will rest." Cassis nodded her head in approval, seeing Loekor pick Maloc up, carrying him as he would a baby.

Bursting through the wall of grass, they luxuriated in the cool breeze as it dried the sweaty rivulets till they were nothing but dirt-stained trails mapping their bodies. Finding a stream, they washed off the grime, sweat, and blood they had accumulated while crossing the plains.

"Should we risk a camp here?" asked Loekor, not liking the idea of being caught in the open.

"Yes, I think we will be safe here, for this night anyway. But then, is there a safe place to be found now?" Cassis answered. She sat brooding over the small fire she had kindled, worry creasing her brow as she stared into the flames' depths.

Splashing out of the stream, Maloc approached the small camp, much refreshed from his bath in the cold water while cursing the many insect bites dotting his arms and head. "How much further to Mount Kan?" he asked, crossing his legs and sitting between his two traveling companions, who at the moment were staring into the fire, each lost in their thoughts.

"We should be there on the morrow," answered Cassis, looking up and staring into the small forest of trees bordering the other side of the small stream, a feeling of being watched coming over her. Straining her ears and eyes, she could see nothing but trees, although she was sure they were being watched. "Unless, my dear Maloc, we meet with a mishap, which is very likely, being we are close to the mountain."

Maloc's heart sank at the thought of imminent danger. He sat in silence, absentmindedly prodding the fire with a stick, his mind racing with worst-case scenarios. Was he really ready to face whatever lay ahead?

"Then we must keep a wary eye out," said Loekor, rising and stretching his frame. He retrieved his bow and quiver of arrows and gave Cassis a knowing look, as if he too felt the danger close by. With one last look in Cassis' direction, he disappeared into the trees, soon lost to sight.

"Where's Loekor going in such a hurry?" Maloc asked, his voice betraying his anxiety. He had noticed the subtle exchange between Cassis and Loekor, and he couldn't shake the feeling that something was amiss.

"To hunt," she lied. "So that we might have meat."

"Oh," said Maloc, stretching out on the cool grass, hiding his nervousness, while sneaking glances at the forest. "Will we combine our watches this night to see what danger lies before us?"

"The danger may be in our seeing, but I suppose it is a chance we must take."

Loekor stealthily made his way through the forest, throwing glances over his shoulder as he advanced deeper, hearing no sounds save those of his own muffled footfalls. Noticing an opening in the trees ahead, he cautiously approached to find himself in a small clearing. Straining his hearing, he couldn't detect the chirping of birds nor the sounds of buzzing insects that should be abounding here. Sitting down on a fallen tree, he resigned himself to the fact that instead of the hunter, he was now the hunted.

A twig snapping brought him to his hooves, and turning to face the direction the sound had come from, his mouth unhinged as he stared with wide eyes at the visage before him.

"I see that you are surprised, Loekor," sneered the stranger. "What's the matter? Have you never seen yourself before?"

Loekor, recovering, said, "I know not what manner of being you are, but it could present a problem being there are two of us."

The stranger grew enraged at the casualness of Loekor's remark. "I think, horned one, it is a problem that may be easily solved," saying this, he bellowed, lowered his head, and charged across the clearing, intent upon skewering Loekor, who was already moving to meet the charge.

Loekor easily sidestepped the mirror image's charge, tripping him as he did so. A yell of rage shook the air as Loekor's look-a-like gained his legs, the dust still settling around him as he fastened his gaze on Loekor, the color of his eyes changing to a deep red, not masking the hate that lay behind them. "You are fast, Loekor. Faster than I would have thought for a creature your size. But die, will you!"

"I do not think so, ugly one," replied Loekor, seeing beyond the mask, seeing the evil that dwelled within, hiding behind a body-suit made up to look like him. "If that is the best you can do in a charge, I would be willing to let the youngest of my people challenge you. It would make good practice in case they ever had need to defend themselves." Seeing the creature's rage intensified till it seemed to shimmer before him, Loekor crouched, waiting, hoping the rage would blind his opponent into making a mistake, so that he might find an opening and finish the contest.

"You talk well for one that is as good as dead," hissed the figure circling Loekor, stooping down till he was almost on all fours as he looked for his opening.

"My death must bother you, for if not, you would not keep repeating it." Loekor, getting an idea, backed toward the trees till he felt the bark biting at his back.

"Do you run, horned one? It will do you no good."

"Run," stammered Loekor. "No, indeed. I just thought I might rest against this tree. You see, this game is starting to bore me, and I grow weary of it."

Howling with rage, the apparition charged, his hooves

thundering upon the ground as he bore down on Loekor, who still leaned against the tree, seemingly unconcerned. At the last possible moment, Loekor stepped aside, grabbing the being by the shoulders, helping him build even more momentum as he struck the tree, giving it cause to bend, groaning, almost double at the impact, showering leaves as well as dead twigs down on the figure lying prone at its base.

Loekor, knowing the being was hurt badly, bent down close to the stranger's mouth as it opened to speak, but instead of speech, only a gurgling sound issued from the mouth as blood dribbled down the side of its face, the neck broken. Even as Loekor looked, the red eyes glazed over. "Remember, wherever it is you go foul one, it was by thine own hand that sent you there." Standing, he noticed the figure on the ground losing its solid form, till at last it was a foul-smelling cloud inching its way into the currents of air.

Striding back into the forest, he noticed several animals gallivanting in its cool shade, no longer hiding. Staring upwards, he saw birds alight on the branches overhead, singing their songs. Feeling something strike his shoulder, he again looked skyward, and spotted a large black bird glaring balefully at him through red eyes.

"Gone, but not forgotten, huh?" The bird hearing this squawked several times before taking wing.

"Such language," said Loekor, reaching up and knocking the bird dropping from his shoulder. Whistling, he made his way back to camp.

Approaching the outer fringe of trees, Loekor saw his two companions much as he had left them, huddled around the fire, munching on the fruit they had gathered earlier. Raising a hoof to step out from the trees, a splashing in the stream gave him pause, freezing him in place. Letting a few seconds pass, he slowly turned his head in the direction the sound had come from, and spied a magnificent deer watering. He felt relief washing over him as he let the pent-up breath he had been holding escape from him in a long sigh.

The deer hearing this raised its proud head, scenting the air, stamping its hooves in challenge. Receiving no reply, it dashed headlong down the shallow stream, disappearing around a bend.

The two figures standing by the small fire had a worried look on their faces as they watched in the direction of the deer's retreat, missing the approach of Loekor till he was almost upon them, causing them to jump a second time.

"Oh, it is you," said Maloc, breathing heavily, the fright on his face apparent. "Why did you not shoot the stag? His meat would have been sweet."

Loekor, sitting down heavily, replied, "Cousin."

"Oh."

It was all Loekor could do not to burst out laughing, happy to be alive and joking, instead of lying dead from his adventure in the forest. Cassis, seeing the jest, kept her silence. "Was there good hunting in the forest?"

"Yes, very good hunting," replied Loekor. Maloc looked perplexed and asked, "Then where is the meat?" Seeing the somber look pass between Loekor and Cassis, he let his question go unanswered, growing silent and munching on the fruit that had until now, lay forgotten in his hand.

Finishing the fruit, Cassis contemplated the gathering darkness battling with the light for control of the site. "It is time." Withdrawing a leather pouch from her robe, she sprinkled the contents over the fire, causing it to fizzle and crackle before a dark cloud of smoke wound its way upward, staying just a few inches above the fire instead of being chased away by the slight breeze. "Come, Maloc, sit beside me." Doing so, they both concentrated on the smoke.

"I see nothing but a black void. This is a bad sign."

"I do not think it is a bad sign, Maloc, but I believe it proves that the Dark One is worried about our presence, or else he would not counter our spell. Indeed, he would want us to see what goes on so that he might gloat. As it is, I fear we will see nothing this night. What is your...?" She left the question unasked as she followed Loekor's eyes, staring transfixed at two huge red orbs hovering just over their heads.

"Ahhh." Maloc fell back, stunned at the twin apparition.

"For you, foul one," said Cassis, throwing a pinch of the powder from the bag in the eyes' direction.

A bright flash stronger than the sun's glare blinded the group, and a howl rent the air, piercing their hearing, giving them cause to cover their ears.

"He knows, for sure."

"Yes," Maloc agreed, still shaking.

Loekor disappeared into the darkness, his senses on high alert. He didn't know what he was looking for, but he knew he would recognize it when he saw it. He moved silently, carefully scanning his surroundings for any sign of danger.

CHAPTER FOURTEEN
The Battle of the Bluff

Grimdom's hand rose slowly, fingers outstretched and stark against the starless sky. But the darkness was absolute, a thick cloak that shrouded even his own hand from view. He could barely make out the figures of his fellow elves around him, let alone the path ahead. With a deep breath, he pressed his fingers to his lips and gave a shrill whistle. The sound pierced the stillness, echoing through the night. As one, the line of silent marchers halted, their feet grinding to a stop in the soft earth. Grimdom waited, his senses attuned to the night, until at last he heard the faint sound of scurrying feet. Another whistle, and the scouts returned, their shapes materializing out of the darkness. Grimdom lowered his hand and addressed the group. "We rest, but first we must station guards on our perimeter."

"I would find it hard to rest now, Grimdom," said Therseus. "If it is alright?"

Acknowledging Therseus, Grimdom sent him out into the blackness with another elf. They were sent out in pairs.

"Just a little further," a high musical voice whispered. "By those boulders. They will guard our back from attack," Theena said.

Therseus stumbled in the darkness, his foot catching on a hidden root. He flailed his arms, but then he felt a firm grip on his arm, steadying him. Looking up, he saw Theena's face, her eyes shining with concern. Standing quietly, they could discern the night sounds all around them, so they worried little about the noise they had made.

"I thank you," whispered Therseus. He explained, "I am not used to traveling in the darkness."

"Feel the ground with your feet. Let them be your eyes."

"I will try," said Therseus, wondering about the elf he was with. His curiosity got the better of him. "By the sound of your voice, I judge you to be young."

"Yes, by elfish standards, I am considered young. If you are judging from my whispered voice, it may be because I am a she-elf."

Therseus gasped for breath, his chest tight with shock. He had never imagined that there could be a she-elf warrior.

Hearing his quick intake of breath, the elf asked, "I hope it does not offend you, me being a she-elf?"

"No... Of course not. I will admit that it caught me unaware."

"Is there not a female warrior in your tribe?"

"Not that I know of," answered Therseus, still dumbfounded at finding a she-elf in this band of brave warriors. "What are you called?"

"I am called Theena. That is enough talk for now. Let us watch so that we may not be surprised. We will have our chance to talk later if you wish."

"I would like that very much," whispered Therseus.

The night wore on without incident. Therseus had almost fallen asleep when he was startled awake by a chorus of bird whistles. "Come. They want us back at the camp."

Shaking the damp night air off, Therseus followed Theena, amazed at her ability to move quickly and quietly through the darkness, easily threading her way back to the main camp. Soon, the rich scent of cooking food wafted towards Therseus, making his stomach growl. He could smell roasted meat, herbs, and spices, and his mouth watered.

Theena chuckled, her musical laughter ringing in the darkness. "You must learn to move quietly, Therseus," she said. Therseus felt a flush of embarrassment spread across his face, but he kept his head down, hoping the darkness would conceal his shame.

The two walking into the camp noticed some new associates.

"Therseus, over here," Grimdom called out. "I'd like you to meet someone."

Stepping through and over the elves squatting in a haphazard circle, eating their late dinner, he finally fought his way to Grimdom. "Therseus, this is Alnap. He and his band have been following your people."

The tall, sparse elf regarded Therseus for several moments before saying anything. "Your people are not far from here. They are camped as we are, waiting for first light."

"Are they alright?" stuttered Therseus.

"They are as well as can be expected. At least there have been no killings," he added as an afterthought.

"Then why are we just sitting here?" Therseus exclaimed, frustration rising in his chest. "We should go free them!"

"At this time, it would be foolish," replied Grimdom. "We must plan. If we rushed in there with no planning, it is possible we would lose many warriors, and possibly many of your own people before we could free them. I know it is hard to wait, but wait and plan is what we must do. Look here." Squatting down, he picked up a small stick, tracing a crude map on the ground. "If they stay on the trail they follow, they will pass by a large bluff with a river bordering the other side. It is here we will attack." Jabbing the stick into the ground, he looked to Therseus and Alnap, but found no reply forthcoming. "It is agreed then?"

Therseus nodded reluctantly. "You're right. It's just hard to wait."

Clenching and unclenching his hands, Therseus paced around the camp, all thought of food gone.

As they waited, Theena brought Therseus a bowl of stew. "You must eat," she said with a smile. "you wouldn't want our ambush being given away by a growling stomach."

Therseus grinned, feeling his spirits lift. "Thanks," he said, digging into the stew.

Waiting until Therseus had finished eating, Theena said, "Grimdom says we will leave within the hour so that we will have time to set up our ambush."

Therseus slapped his fist against the ground. "That is good news. I hate sitting here doing nothing when I know my people are so near." Feeling something soft, he looked down, seeing Theena's hand resting on top of his own.

"Do not worry, Therseus, it will be alright."

Turning to get his first good look at Theena, he felt his heart give a lurch as he looked deep into the blue eyes, merriment dancing in their depths as well as concern.

Reaching out, he touched the golden hair spilling down over her shoulders, which was so recently held captive under her cap. "Why... why, you are beautiful." He let his eyes drop to the pouting mouth and finely boned nose.

She turned from his stare, content to let her hand rest upon his. The warmth flowing back and forth like an electrical current.

Just as they lay in wait, they heard the sounds of goblins herding prisoners. Therseus's anger boiled inside him, but he knew he had to wait for Grimdom's signal to attack.

As they lay in silence, Theena's hand found his, offering a small comfort. Therseus's heart quickened at the touch, and he squeezed her hand in return. They waited together, listening to the distant cries of the prisoners, their nerves stretched to the breaking point.

Soon, they could hear the cries of people in bondage, the screams as whips were brought into play to hurry them along.

Therseus felt his stomach knot at hearing the goblin's curses at his people. Lying there, he could barely control himself, his anger rising until it was like a red film before his eyes, his heart pumping blood hot in his veins. It was all he could do to stop himself from charging down the bluff to confront the goblins. Tensed like a coiled spring, he waited, grinding his teeth, each second stretched out until it seemed like days had passed.

Grimdom raised his arm to give the order to attack, but before a word could leave his mouth, the sky above them opened as if wounded, pouring forth a blinding white light that was soon followed by a wailing, as if the sky itself was screaming from the pain the opening had produced. It seemed that all the lightning found in the skies had gathered here, striking the ground and searing all that it touched in retaliation.

"Spread out, take cover!" screamed Grimdom, even though his words carried no further than his own hearing.

"Fools!" bellowed a voice from the skies. "Did you think it would be so easy?" The voice faded into laughter as the lightning bolts continued to rain down upon the ground, bringing death and utter destruction to all that were struck by its fury.

Therseus raised himself to one knee, looking toward Grimdom, and saw him wildly gesticulating his arms. Blinking his eyes rapidly to clear them of smoke, he stood up in the confusion, intent upon reaching the elvish leader. Taking two steps in Grimdom's direction, he was blinded by a bright flash, the ground below him vibrating, causing him to stumble and drop to one knee. Recovering himself, he again looked toward where Grimdom had been standing but saw only a smoking crater. "No, no!" he screamed, staring wildly around, seeing elves disappear in blinding flashes of light.

"Theena!" he screamed, turning and bumping into an elf clawing at a wooden shaft protruding from his chest. With anger blinding him to all else, he stole to the edge of the bluff and saw several goblins shooting arrows randomly to the top in hopes of hitting one of their attackers. Therseus could see the twisted, sneering faces of the goblins below as they launched their deadly arrows. He felt their malice like a tangible thing, a cruel energy that sought to snuff out the lives of his comrades from afar."

A feeling of tranquility came over him as he accepted his death. Calmly, he slid his quiver of arrows from his shoulder. He let loose his first arrow and felt a dark joy in getting some revenge for the fallen elves as he watched his target squirm on the ground, clutching at the arrow buried in his stomach. He let loose two, three, four arrows and smiled grimly as each found its mark. Therseus rose to his feet, his quiver now nearly empty. With a fierce cry, he charged towards the goblins below, heedless of the danger. The goblins, startled by the sudden movement, fired a volley of arrows at the dark figure illuminated by the lightning flashes. He felt something slam into his shoulder, knocking him to the ground even as the pain in his leg registered another arrow finding its mark.

Raising himself on his elbows, he stared at the shaft sticking from his leg as he gingerly felt around the arrow buried in his shoulder, not believing he was still alive. Determined, he dragged himself to the bluff's edge and looked down at the goblins milling about, content with the knowledge they were in no danger from above.

Turning his head, he looked behind himself, but all he could see was blackness, not even a star to shine its pitiless light down on the carnage below. Concentrating his ears, he could hear nothing, the wind circling the battle unwilling to disturb the dead. Smelling the air, his nostrils were attacked by the stench of burnt flesh. "No, no," he cried to himself. Then anger took him into its folds. A burning anger that could not be sated. Standing up, he looked down on the shadows milling about. "I live!" he shouted.

The goblins looked up, startled at first, but seeing no target to loose their arrows on, they lost interest as it grew quiet and continued their march toward Mount Kan, with Therseus muttering curses at their backs.

With the goblins gone, herding the people as if they were cattle, he cried in frustration, knowing they thought him dead. He himself knew this would soon be true enough. Laying back, he gazed up into the morning sky, the sun just breaching the horizon. Therseus gritted his teeth against the waves of pain that wracked his body, but a choked sob escaped his lips. He reached for the arrow in his shoulder, his fingers trembling with the effort. 'I'm sorry,' he whispered to no one in particular, the tears streaming down his face. Through half-conscious eyes, he spied a shadow looming over him. But turning his tear-stained face was too much for his tortured body, and he gratefully blacked out.

"What is that?" asked Loekor, standing and shielding his eyes from the bright flashes of light.

"I fear it is the dark one," replied Cassis. "We must make haste to Mount Kan. Without the scepter, we are almost powerless to stop him."

"What of your own powers?" inquired Maloc.

"A thousand years ago, I would have challenged him, but now —"

"Who does the dark one attack?" Maloc asked.

"I fear—" Cassis stared at Loekor, seeing the question also on his face. "It must be Grimdom."

"Grimdom," echoed Loekor. "But Therseus is with Grimdom!"

"I know," said Cassis, the anguish causing a catch to come from her choked voice.

"Why, why!? We must we go to aid them!"

Cassis placed herself in front of Loekor. "It is too late."

"It is my fault," choked Loekor. "If only I had left him where we met!"

Cassis placed a gentle hand on Loekor's arm. "It was his destiny. Be happy with the knowledge he died fighting evil like a true warrior."

"Perhaps Grimdom's lot still live," said Maloc.

"It would be hard to imagine anything living through that," replied Cassis. "If only the dark forces would not block our way, then we could know for sure. Let us just hope their deaths were fast and painless."

Loekor stumbled away from the fire, his shoulders slumped in grief. He collapsed against a nearby tree, the bark rough against his cheek. In the darkness, he wept silently for his lost friend, unable to shake the image of Therseus falling to the goblins' arrows. Maloc tried to make his way to Loekor, but Cassis stopped him. "Leave him to his grief." They passed the night in silence, the only sounds being the chirping of insects and the crackling of the small campfire.

CHAPTER FIFTEEN

The Battle on the Plains of Leon.

The sun beat down relentlessly as King Illson and his army marched towards the Plains of Leon. The king looked back at his tired soldiers, their metal helms and armor glinting in the harsh light. Halting his mount, he raised his arm signaling the army to halt and rest, knowing the sun and choking dust were fast sapping their strength. Shrugging his shoulders, he felt the leather bindings holding his armor bite deeper into his already raw shoulders as he spurred his mount toward a distant rolling hillock.

Reaching up to remove his helm, he felt a shower of sweat rain down, temporarily blinding his already stinging eyes, while his steed's gait jarred him to his very bones. Arriving at the top of the hillock, he swiped the sweat from his eyes with the back of his mailed hand, scraping the sunburnt skin. Cursing himself for this self-inflicted pain, he opened his eyes to observe what lay before him and felt his stomach drop at the sight.

Stretched for miles ahead lay an ocean of purple-skinned goblins, the sun winking off bits and pieces of their armor as they marched forward, stomping and trampling any trace of life from the beautiful plains.

"To conquer an army," he chuckled to himself. "This has to be a jest, perhaps a trick of the heat and dust." Wiping his eyes again, he counted row upon row of what he imagined grim-faced marchers, but soon gave up seeing the marchers stretched beyond his vision. "What would my army think if they could see what I see?" answering himself, "They would probably retreat back to the city. No," he admonished himself. "They would fight to the last elf." King Illson cursed himself for leading his army into such a hopeless battle. He shook the thought from his mind and galloped back to his troops to prepare them for the fight ahead.

He could not help wondering if Lark had seen the purple ocean pouring across the plains and perhaps even now retreated with his dark elves. Pushing this thought back, he cursed himself as he imagined Lark would if he knew what had crossed the young king's mind.

Pulling his steed up in a whirl of dust, he found his captains anxiously waiting for his report. Stepping down, he paced back and forth, his hand clasped behind his back, searching for words that would send elves to a certain death. Finally, he turned, looking each captain in the eye. "I fear we will find no glory on this day." Stooping down, he plucked a blade of grass. "The goblins' numbers are as many as the blades of grass that cover this plain." He paused, searching the eyes of his captains before him for a sign of weakness or fear, wanting to share the emotions that battled inside of himself. Seeing none, he continued. "We stand before this vast army—the only obstacle in their path. With our army out of the way, it would be easy for them to conquer our small city, and mayhap this world."

"What of the goblin ambassador?" interjected a captain. "I thought their intention was to join us."

"I fear it may be treachery on their general's part, perhaps to lure us away from the safety of the city walls. Of course, I cannot be sure, but I have seen—"

"If it is battle they want, it is a battle they will receive, and one they will not soon forget," said the captain.

"I think one of the first things we should do is send ten good elves back to the city so that the elves may be warned of this menace and to evacuate the city if need be." Seeing the captain's questioning look, he sent them to the same hillock, knowing the sight would be better seen than told of.

Watching the captains gesturing, he knew them to be planning offensive and defensive actions as well as the armies' positions. Though they knew as well as he that the battle ahead was hopeless, it swelled his chest with pride at the sight of these brave leaders as a silent tear traced itself down his boyish face.

Returning, the grim-faced captains encircled the king. "It is as you say," said a young captain not much older than Illson. "I think it would be wise to send the ten elves back with a severe warning for the elves that were left to defend the city."

"Sire," intoned another captain. "I do not think it would be wise for a direct frontal attack. If we engaged them in battle, they would soon have us encircled, then it would only be a matter of time, even with Lark flanking them. There are just too many of them."

"What do you suggest?" asked King Illson, leveling his gaze at the captain, hoping his voice did not betray the false hope he felt.

"We need to hit and run, sire. A running battle is our only chance. We won't defeat them, but we will hurt them mightily. At this point, it is all we can hope for." There was a muttering of agreement from the other captains.

The captains divided their troops into groups of five hundred and prepared for battle. Thus divided, the captains hoped to keep a continual rain of death falling on the goblins, halting or at the least slowing their steady advance. They figured this was the best plan, although they knew it would not take long to exhaust their supply of arrows, and who knows, by then, perhaps they could find a supply of rocks to throw. They jested between themselves.

Having dispatched scouts, they had not long to wait before they received word a small envoy had detached itself from the main body, thus giving the king and two captains cause to go and meet them.

Topping the rise, they had not far to go before seeing the ambassador who had paid them a visit along with several goblins in mismatched armor flanking him, walking briskly in their direction.

As the goblins drew closer, one of the captains said, "Sire, if my eyes do not deceive me, that is elvish armor they wear, or at least. . .part of it." Gripping the hilt of his sword, he cursed under his breath, knowing where the armor had come from. Bitterness stabbed at the captain's heart, knowing with certainty that elves would relinquish their armor only upon death.

"Easy, Captain," said King Illson, noticing the grip that threatened to unleash the sword at his side and seeing the hate pour forth from the captain's eyes. "Let us wait to see what word they bring us." A grudge carried a thousand years, he mused while casting glances from his captain to the goblins who were now almost upon them. How they have hidden these feelings from me, and I their king thought I knew them.

The trio of Elves stood atop a small hill, watching as a group of goblins approached. The ambassador, flanked by two goblins in mismatched armor, walked briskly toward them.

As they drew closer, one of the goblins stepped forward, sneering. "Greetings, Elves. I am Captain Klock, and I have been sent by our great General Grildon to demand your surrender."

"And what happened to his offer of joining the Elves?" He stared levelly at the ambassador, his gaze unwavering.

"Consider it a jest." The goblin captain smiled at what he thought was funny, in his twisted way of thinking. "Can you not see the humor in this?" Changing his smile into a snarl, he continued. "You've already seen, our numbers are great, and for your pitiful army to fight us will bring about your own doom." Pausing, he sneered, "I think it would be wise for you to lay down your arms, and perhaps my general will spare the Elves their lives this day."

The ambassador shifted nervously, his eyes darting between the elf king and Captain Klock. "Wait," he said, his voice shaking. "There must be some mistake. Our general promised to join forces with the Elves, not attack them." Captain Klock's sneer deepened. "The general changed his mind. And he wants your armor, too," he added, addressing the ambassador. "He says he's tired of looking at your ugly face."

"Your leader will pay dearly for this breach of promise," answered the king.

The goblin captain, unable to contain himself any longer, screamed, "Slay them!"

Hearing this, rage filled the young king. Spurring his mount forward, he skewered the screaming goblin on the norn's horn while drawing his sword and looking into the vile face before him. His sword was a silver blur of motion, decapitating the flailing goblin and enveloping himself and his mount in a geyser of foul-smelling blood. Wiping the blood from his eyes, he looked from left to right, staying his sword after seeing the bloody havoc wreaked by his captains on the remaining goblins. The last goblin, the ambassador, stood with his legs unwilling to move. Seeing the king's approach, he closed his eyes, knowing it was his time but unwilling to face it. Feeling something press against his chest, his heart constricted in fear. Then something miraculous happened. A voice.

"Hear me, goblin," said a quiet, dignified voice. "I believe you innocent of this vile deceit, and for this reason, and this reason alone, I shall spare your miserable life. If goblins give thanks, let it be for Cassis, for it was she who spoke for you in my court. Tell your leader to make ready for battle."

The goblin, squinting through misted eyes, fell to his knees. "I thank you for my life. Your message will be delivered to the general."

"So be it." The king, a grim set to his face, turned his mount, followed by his captains. As the minutes passed and insects grew quiet in expectation while carnivorous birds circled high overhead.

Returning to his troops, the king found three of Lark's elves waiting for him. "Lark wishes to know if we are to engage the enemy," asked the leader of the black-clad trio.

Taking off his helm, the king wearily drew his hand across his eyes. "I have already issued a challenge." Taking a sip of the water offered to him by one of his soldiers, he continued. "We have no choice but to engage them in battle."

All three elves broke into wide grins. "A wise decision, sire." Bowing, the three elves disappeared through the waiting troops.

"A decision," thought the king, watching the backs of the retreating elves, "but a wise decision? I do not think so." He sent word to ready the troops, and soon the air was filled with a general grunting as bows were strung and arrows loosened in their quivers, the sounds of war soon approaching.

CHAPTER SIXTEEN
The Chosen One and the Staff of Power

The large bear-like animal stood on its hind legs, scenting the air while warily keeping an eye on the figures huddled around a small fire. Sensing danger, it reluctantly ambled around the small group, casting glances over its shoulder and letting a low growl issue from its chest.

"Who was that?" asked Maloc, jumping to his feet.

"Easy, Maloc," instructed Cassis. "It is just a nocturnal animal."

"Of course." After one more look into the darkness, Maloc resumed his seat. "Of course, it was," he mumbled to himself, feeling the night's chill dampness clinging to him like an unwelcome second skin.

Loekor rose, stretching his powerful body, and peered into the darkness where the animal had disappeared. He turned to his companions and said, "I'll gather more wood and take a closer look. I'm certain there's nothing to fear, but it's always better to be cautious." He gave Maloc a reassuring look, then nodded to Cassis before disappearing into the darkness.

"I think he still mourns for young Therseus," said Maloc, watching Loekor's broad back retreating into the night and noticing the way the powerful shoulders sagged. "If only I could see, then we would know Therseus' destiny as well as our own, mayhap."

Loekor silently made his way through a thicket until he last spied a boulder, and it was this he sat upon while pondering the events that led him here. Deep in thought with his head resting on his upturned palm, he failed to notice the firefly lazily spiraling towards him. Letting his mind flow through the river of his past life, he reflected on the reason for his being when he felt an intrusion upon his mind. A soft, feathery touch, not uncomfortable nor unsettling but surprising. He felt a slight, unexplainable tickling, but he could not judge why he knew it was of no danger to him. He felt himself falling into blackness and almost screamed. When it seemed his sight had returned, he looked downward and saw himself slowly descending into soft, billowy clouds with a field of many-colored flowers below this. As he got even closer to the field, he saw a lone figure standing among the flowers. A figure with a white beard dressed in a loose, flowing robe of many colors. Feeling as light as a feather being tossed in the wind, he settled gently on the ground. The robed figure scarcely three feet away. The old man extended his hand in friendship, and Loekor grasped his arm.

"Welcome, Loekor of the Horned Ones," he said in a high tinkling voice. "I am the wizard Soren."

"How — why?" Loekor stammered, struggling to comprehend the surreal experience.

"I will explain it all to you, Loekor. That's why I have brought you here." Placing a hand on Loekor's shoulder, he beckoned him to walk with him. "First, this is a place of power, and not your imagination. It is just as real as I am."

Loekor found himself brought to a high mountain meadow as he was led across it to find himself staring down into a broad valley. A huge shadow crossed the ground, accompanied by a loud roar, and looking up, he saw a large dragon of burnished gold. Looking around wildly for a hiding place, he felt a reassuring pat on his arm.

"Do not fear, Loekor." Leading Loekor, Soren pointed to a natural stairway, and it was these they descended to the valley far below. Reaching a small, placid lake, they sat on a wooden bench carved with many runes on its surface. Loekor stared at these while waiting for Soren to speak.

"Let us rest, Loekor, for I am old and tire easily these days." Moving his hands in articulate gestures, he produced two goblets of a fine, sweet nectar.

"How — ?"

"It is a small trick, my friend," Soren replied, taking a sip and staring out over the silvery water.

Loekor sipped the sweet liquid, relishing its pleasant taste as he watched the fireflies dance over the water's surface. Soon, they were flying around himself and Soren. As he watched, one settled on his arm, and his eyes grew wide at seeing it wasn't a firefly at all, but a small, miniature being silver in color with clear, crystalline wings. The small creature gave a tentative smile while preening its two delicate antennae, then it was airborne, dancing back over the water to join its comrades in play.

"Things are as they seem," chuckled Soren, seeing the surprised look on Loekor's face.

"This is indeed a magical place. A wonderful place," said Loekor, relaxing in tranquility.

Soren's face became a mask of seriousness as he turned to Loekor. "I am glad you think so, Loekor, for you are the chosen one to preserve its beauty as well as the other world from which you come."

"How, how am I to do this?"

"The scepter, Loekor. It holds immense power," Soren explained, taking a deep breath. "It is the key to unlocking the secrets of this world and bringing its power to your own. It would be hard to explain, but I can tell you that this world runs parallel to your own, and there is a Dark Lord who seeks to conquer both. His world also runs parallel to yours, and it is to his world you must send him back to. The scepter is the key to achieving this. If he obtains the scepter, he will unleash horrors beyond your imagination."

"I am merely a Horned One— no more."

Laying his hand on Loekor's shoulder, he turned Loekor to face him. Loekor looked at the lined, craggy face and the soft, understanding eyes. His heart going out to Loekor.

"I can truthfully say I do not understand the powers that be, Loekor, but I do know that you have been chosen to take up the scepter and rid your world of this invader. Your destiny was set in motion long ago in ancient times and has led all the way to this point."

"How am I to retrieve the scepter?" choked Loekor, his emotions boiling within him.

"Let your inner self guide you, Loekor, for even now the scepter builds power in anticipation of your coming. It is a heavy burden you carry, but carry it you must."

A rainbow of many colors shot from the surface of the water, its vibrant hues arching across the sky before resting in the high meadow. Loekor gasped in amazement at the spectacle, noticing small, crystalline lights flickering beneath the rainbow's surface, intensifying its brilliance.

"It is time for you to return," said Soren, standing and gesticulating his arms.

Loekor stood and unconsciously ducked his head, hearing a cross between the roar of an avalanche and the shriek of a tempest. "What—" he managed to say before he lost his voice at the sight spiraling downward to them.

"He is an ally, Loekor."

The strange beast landed not far from them, spreading its golden wings once more before tucking them next to its tawny hide. Raking its huge claws across the ground, it beat a loud rhythm with its tail, waiting.

Grasping his hand, Soren led the protesting Loekor closer to the beast. "This is Auk."

The creature looked out at them through golden eyes, opening its cavernous beak and emitting a chirp of greeting.

"Auk, this is Loekor, the chosen one. I wish you to return him safely to his own world."

The beast nodded its head once in answer, its coal-black mane brushing the ground.

"Come, Loekor, let's make friends," Soren said, gesturing toward the gryphon.

Loekor placed a trembling hand on the beast's shoulder, liking the velvety feel. The beast turned its head, looking down at Loekor and making a chirping sound of greeting.

"How is he to take me back?"

In answer, the gryphon lay on its belly so Loekor might mount its broad back.

"You will ride the winds, Loekor."

Loekor felt himself falling through blackness once more. A jolting fall brought reality back. Getting up, he saw that he had fallen from the boulder he had been sitting on. "Perhaps a dream," he thought to himself, looking up in time to see Auk's broad wings cutting across the bright disc of the moon.

Rubbing his head and still not quite able to believe what had happened to him, he stared down at himself and a small cry of awe escaped him upon seeing a robe of many colors flowing over his large frame. "I guess he wanted to be sure I didn't confuse him for a dream," Loekor chuckled to himself. As he made his way back, he was surprised at the lightness of the robes, for they felt as though they weighed no more than the air around him. Approaching the stream he had crossed earlier, a peculiar light caught his attention, reflecting in the dark waters. Looking down, he saw his antlers reflecting in the water; they were now as white as polished ivory with an eerie inner glow. Stooping down, he ran his hands through the water, feeling its coolness while gazing at his reflection. "Destiny calls," he thought to himself, and with these thoughts, he returned to the small camp.

CHAPTER SEVENTEEN
A Prophecy Fulfilled

Maloc was first to see him approaching and muffled a cry seeing the way he illuminated the path before him, the long flowing robe with its colors shifting in the soft light emanating from his horns. The Horned one had shoulder length hair its dark curly waves enhanced with soft silvery streaks. As he drew closer Maloc stifled a cry and took flight hiding behind a large boulder.

"It is only I Maloc, Loekor."

"You are wrong Loekor," spoke Cassis rising and bowing before Loekor. "It is as it was foretold. The chosen one." Looking up to the stars she spied what appeared to be a new star shimmering in a soft brilliance.

Maloc not quite believing what his eyes told him listened to his heart and crawled out of hiding from behind the boulder on unsteady knee's bowed kissing the hem of Loekor's robe.

"My friends do not pay tribute to me, for without you I would not be here now. It will be us and not just I that will recover the scepter." Squatting down by the fire he continued, "With the scepter we will destroy the Dark one send him back from whence he came and avenge our allies." He almost chocked on the last words as thoughts of Therseus came to him wishing he was with them here now.

Maloc and Cassis sat across from Loekor, watching the power he had acquired emanate from him, looking much like the hot desert air rising in shimmering clear waves.

"Tomorrow," Loekor mumbled, drifting into sleep.

Cassis motioned for Maloc to rest, and as he settled down, she made her way to the boulder where he had been hiding earlier. Levitating her small body, she perched on the boulder and looked out towards the night sounds and the coming of a new day. Despite the gravity of the situation, she found it hard to suppress the excitement she felt, and the corners of her mouth tugged upward in a smile. "All is not lost," she whispered to herself.

Meanwhile, in troubled slumber, Loekor's mind was filled with visions of the battle at the Elvish Kingdom. He knew that time was of the essence if there was any hope of saving them. As he slept, his mind raced, and he opened an inner eye, seeing with wonder the scenes unfolding below him. He watched as hundreds upon hundreds of tiny fires dotted the rolling hills surrounding the Kingdom. "Are we already too late?" he wondered as he drifted closer to the ground. Despite the urgency of the situation, he remained asleep, his body growing light as he sailed upon silent night winds towards the Kingdom.

A goblin sentry, drowsy with sleep, saw a blue sphere out of the corner of his eye and shaking his head to clear it of grogginess, turned to stare at the sphere hovering a scant two feet above the ground. Cautiously, he approached the floating sphere with sword raised, ready to strike, when a blue spark danced from the now pulsing sphere to strike the tip of his sword, sending an electrifying shock down its length. The goblin shrieking in pain fell down, all senses leaving him as his fellow goblins made their way to the commotion.

"The blue ball, the blue ball," muttered the goblin as he was carried to one of the many campfires.

A goblin sentry made his way to his captain, who at the time was staring down at the prostrate form of the fallen goblin, who still mumbled about a blue ball.

"We found nothing, sir," growled the goblin.

"I dare not disturb the General without proof of some kind. Back to your post, sentry, and do not disturb me again without this proof."

The blue sphere danced across the night sky until it was within the walls of the Elvish Kingdom.

"Stay your hand," said a wall guard. "If it meant harm, it would have already struck."

The two elves stared in fascination at the pulsing blue sphere.

"Summon your King," a voice rang inside their heads, shaking them from their almost hypnotic state.

"Do as it bids." The elf who first spotted the orb soon disappeared into the city's shadows.

King Illson, his face haggard, soon appeared, followed by several more elves, all brandishing weapons. Opening his mouth to question, he forgot his tongue, seeing the blue sphere hovering above the ground.

Swallowing hard, he approached even closer. "What--what are you?" he asked, motioning the elves behind him to stay back.

"It is I, sire, Loekor," a voice coming from the sphere said.

"What, how!?"

"It's not important, sire. What is important is how you fare."

"I have but a thousand warriors left," he choked. "Of Lark and his forces, I cannot say. We found ourselves surrounded by the goblin army, and if not for Lark opening a way for us, we surely would have all perished. As it was, the fighting was bloody, but it was fought valiantly. We retreated here, where you find us now."

"Without the scepter, there is little I can do, sire, but I ask you to hold your Kingdom until I return."

"We--we will try, although soon I fear all will be lost. Is there nothing..."

"I will do what I can, sire."

The sphere rose into the night air, slowly drifting over the goblins' encampment.

The king and many warriors watched from the top of the walls' protection. The blue sphere slowly grew, its illumination growing as bright as the brightest day, till last it burst, raining down thousands of miniatures of itself. Each tiny blue sphere burst into flame as they touched the ground, tents, and goblins, causing a mass of confusion as goblins beat at the fires enveloping them, as well as the surrounding countryside of their encampment.

A loud cheer came from the direction of the Elvish Kingdom. A silent cheer came from Lark and what was left of his own meager troops as they watched from a distance.

"We will hold," said the King, watching in grim satisfaction at the havoc created by the blue sphere.

Waking, Loekor saw Cassis intently staring at him from her perch.

"How is it with the elves?" asked Cassis.

Rising and stretching tired limbs, he turned his attention to Cassis. "How is it you know?"

"Have you forgotten, Loekor? I am Cassis, Witch of the Blue Forest!"

"The elves have lost many, and even as we speak, have taken a stand behind the walls of their Kingdom, unless it was a dream I lived."

"It was no dream, Loekor. Soren has bestowed powers upon you that even I know nothing of."

"How is it, Cassis, that I use this power even though I do not understand it myself?"

"Let your heart guide you, Loekor," answered Cassis, slowly descending to the ground. "It will come to you."

"Maloc," spoke Cassis, "arise, for we have a long day's journey."

Maloc rose, grumbling. "Would it not be easier for you to transport us to Mount Kan, Cassis? I am old, and surely this journey will be the death of me."

"If it were in my power, surely I would do this, old one, but it is not, and I fear if Loekor were to try, it would lead the Dark One directly to us. Until Loekor has the scepter in his possession, he will be no match for the Dark One's power."

"Mayhap there is something I might do," said Loekor, looking at his two tired companions. "Eat and rest till I return." Turning, he stalked into the forest.

"What is it he will do?" asked Maloc, turning his attention to his sore feet, rubbing them while casting a glance in the direction Loekor had taken, wearing a quizzical look.

"I know not what he will do," answered Cassis, "but I trust it will benefit us. For now, let us do as he bids and eat while we wait for his return."

While engaged in their eating, a loud roar reverberated through the air, shaking leaves from the nearby trees and sending small animals scurrying in a mad flight for safety.

Jumping to his feet, Maloc grabbed Cassis by a loose flowing sleeve. "We must hide," he stammered. "We must run."

Cassis stood her ground as the heavy tread came closer, accompanied by a roar that would topple a brick wall and cause the stoutest of heart to flee.

"Run, Cassis!" Maloc shrieked. "It is our only chance! The grackette cares not what it eats, and a more fearsome animal there is not." Maloc pleaded, dancing from one foot to the other, indecision etched on his face. Not wanting to leave Cassis, yet fearing for his own life, his instincts begging him to flee this terrifying menace.

With a loud cracking, two small trees toppled as gigantic furred shoulders bulldozed their way toward the stream. Standing on hind legs, the bear-like creature looked down at the two small figures from its lofty height of twenty feet.

"It is too late," sobbed Maloc, dropping to his knees, waiting for his fate with closed eyes.

The grackette dropped down to all fours, shaking the very ground with its tonnage. Opening a cavernous mouth filled with teeth resembling the nasty short swords so loved by the goblins, it let loose a mighty roar that could be heard by all those within its domain. Raking claws across the ground, it gouged out a massive hole in the ground before beginning its slow advance. A loud whistle gave it pause as it cocked clamshell-shaped ears.

Cassis showed no outward sign of fear, although she could feel her heart beating faster and louder than it had for many years as she stared into the yellow, pupil-less eyes.

"I have returned," hollered Loekor, followed by a smaller version of the behemoth that now sat on its haunches, delicately preening the dark brown fur covering its enormous body.

Maloc chanced opening one eye and felt his heart lurch at being so close to this titan. "Are we alive?" he asked through clenched teeth.

"Yes, we are alive," answered Cassis, grasping Maloc under his arm and helping him to stand on trembling legs.

"This grackette has consented to take us to Mount Kan," said Loekor, reaching up and scratching the beast behind a colossal ear.

"I would rather walk," said Maloc, keeping a wary eye on the beast as he slowly backed away.

"Do not be silly, Maloc. I have befriended this grackette so that we may ride to Mount Kan. It will take a fraction of the time it would take us to walk there."

"A wise choice," spoke Cassis, impressed with Loekor. "And better protection we could not have. I know of nothing or no one that would stand in the way of a grackette—except perhaps the Dark One himself."

CHAPTER EIGHTEEN
The Power of the Scepter

Upon arriving at Mount Kan, Loekor dismissed the grackette and gazed up at the cloud-shrouded peak. "Cassis, I never imagined a mountain like this could exist. How can we start searching for Soren's lost scepter? I don't even know where to begin," Loekor said with a resigned expression, sitting down and folding his hands.

Cassis placed a small hand on his shoulder. "The answer lies within you," she said.

"How? I don't even know where to start," Loekor replied.

"Close your eyes and think of a time when you felt at peace and calm," Cassis instructed.

Bowing his head, he replied, "I will try, Cassis. I will try."

Maloc hurried toward them, but Cassis raised a hand to signal for him to be quiet. She led him away from Loekor, who seemed lost in thought.

"What's wrong?" Cassis asked.

"Goblins, coming this way," Maloc whispered urgently.

"Don't worry. We'll deal with them soon," Cassis replied calmly.

Suddenly, a soft voice whispered in the wind, "Loekor."

Loekor thought back to the kind face of Soren, of the meadow and the valley. He felt at peace with himself while also feeling part of his essence slip away, and it was this that he followed, ignoring all else.

"Come, Maloc, we must hurry." Thus, they followed Loekor as Maloc cast furtive glances behind them, wishing the grackette were still with them.

After half a day's journey, Cassis and Maloc were disappointed. They had covered very little ground, having to cross numerous ravines and gullies etched into this once fiery giant. Even deep within goblin territory, they had not seen even a single patrol, although they were sure they had heard curses borne on the ever-present wind.

"I must rest," gasped Maloc, finding a large boulder and sitting on it, rubbing his bruised feet.

"You are right, Maloc. We must rest." Cassis stared at Loekor's back as it slowly diminished into the distance. "We should be able to wait here for Loekor's return." Reaching into her robe, she brought forth a handful of white powder, which she threw into the air, enveloping herself and Maloc. "This will render us invisible to the goblins," she answered in response to his bewildered expression.

Loekor continued his steep climb, dislodging small rocks with his hooves that echoed their downward course as they danced across the mountain's hard surface until they shattered on the ground far below.

Onward he climbed, drawn upward by a force he could not understand, although he felt the urging getting stronger with every step he took.

A short time later, he found himself on a large outcropping of rock, staring fixedly at a crack etched on the mountain's hard surface, a soft glow emanating from it.

Placing his hands on the crack, he felt, rather than heard, the hum coming from within growing louder and stronger, beckoning him so strongly that he clawed at the unyielding surface.

In desperation, he used his antlers to try and pry the crack open but to no avail.

His senses returning, he sat before it, concentrating all his energies on focusing his mind on the source of energy that waited behind the crack.

The hum grew louder, echoing and reverberating, causing an avalanche of rocks to spill from the mountain's steep sides as dust rose into the air, blanketing all.

An unnatural quiet settled on the mountain as its bucking and heaving came to an end. The crack now an opening, Loekor rose, stepping into the small cavern, his eyes never wavering from the scepter. Approaching it, he timidly reached out his hands, encircling the glowing rod. As his hands made contact, he felt its power coursing through his body. A feeling of oneness with this new power flowed over him, pulling at him and stretching him, not just his mind, but something much deeper than that, something deep to the very core of his being. As the power of the scepter threatened to overtake him, finally, it calmed, softened, and ultimately yielded to him.

Cassis and Maloc found themselves in a difficult situation as the goblins marched their human captives right past them. The goblins stopped only a few feet away, arguing about the best course of action while others prodded and jeered at the prisoners. The women's cries gave great delight to their captors, but Cassis and Maloc couldn't help feeling helpless despite their invisibility

If the goblins had bothered to look up, they would have seen the clouds disrobing the bare mountain peak as they slowly descended toward them. But the goblins were too focused on their prisoners to notice the approaching phenomenon.

Cassis nudged Maloc to guide his gaze upward, hoping he would see the approaching blue light. However, Maloc was already terrified by the goblins' close proximity, and he yelped before Cassis could cover his mouth. In a hoarse whisper, she warned him to be quiet, even as the goblins close to them cast glances in their direction, confusion showing on their faces.

"What was that?" asked a particularly large and ugly goblin, walking over and standing within inches of Maloc and Cassis.

"Perhaps a rabbit," croaked another, poking a sparse bush with his spear point. Soon, however, they were covered in the damp embrace of the cloud, making it impossible to see anything but a pulsing blue light growing ever closer. It was all the ugly goblin could do to keep the rest from bolting away. He cursed them soundly, warning them of the Dark One's anger and his reprisal at disobedience.

"Drop your weapons," a voice thundered.

"Do not listen," warned the ugly goblin, more afraid of the Dark One's anger than some voice shrouded in mist.

The blue light grew stronger, brighter till the sun itself was its only equal as goblins now stood rooted in abject terror. They threw down their weapons so they might cover their eyes from the blinding illumination.

"Give me a bow," screamed their leader, and soon an arrow was notched.

It was then a blue bolt shot from the center of the light, catching the goblin's leader in a sizzling fury. The goblin closest to the commander looked down at the smoldering heap of what was just his commander and let out a blood-chilling scream before bolting headlong down the steep sides with the rest of the goblins in close pursuit.

The men and women stood frozen, unsure of their fates until a voice spoke out from the light. "Stand fast, you are delivered."

They looked toward the light, now a dull pulsing blue, and waited in uncertainty. Soon, the clouds lifted, and the people caught their breath as Loekor stood before them. The robe he wore shimmered in its own radiance, as well as the antlers adorning his head. Spying the scepter, they bowed down, the women weeping again, but this time in joy as the men voiced their thanks.

They were stunned a second time as Cassis and Maloc materialized in front of them.

"Do not be afraid, mortals. It is I, Cassis of the Blue Forest, along with Maloc, the Seer of the Kingdom of Elves." Raising her arm, she continued, "and behold, your deliverer, Loekor of the Horned Ones. The wielder of power. The retainer of the Scepter of Soren."

"The Scepter of Soren," echoed throughout the crowd.

A large man with hair and beard as black as a raven's wing with piercing blue eyes reached down and retrieved an elvish sword. "To serve."

"To serve!" the other men yelled, following the first's example and taking up the discarded arms.

Maloc approached Loekor on wobbly legs. "You actually found it." Kneeling down, he took Loekor's hand, placing it on his shoulder, an elvish expression of servitude.

Cassis stared with pride at Loekor. "I thank you, Cassis."

"No. It is I that should give thanks to you." So saying, she also bowed down.

"Arise, dear friend, for dear friend it shall always be." He looked out over the multitude of people. "We march to the Elvish Kingdom to help them defeat the goblins."

The crowd roared its approval, "death to the goblins." And so it was they marched toward the beleaguered elves.

CHAPTER NINETEEN

The Battle of the Walls: A Last Stand for the Elvish Kingdom

The fires were so numerous that they gave the Elvish Kingdom the appearance of being surrounded by a sea of flame. Elves manning the walls nervously fidgeted with their weapons while looking out over this seemingly endless tide and watching the ghostly apparitions stalking between the red and yellow waves. Hopelessness showed on many of the elven faces, although if one looked deep into their eyes, they would still see the burning resolve never to surrender to the hordes of vile goblins.

King Illson was proud of his warriors and what they had accomplished, etching the deeds and names deep into his memories. He wondered how his father must have felt during the Hundred Year War, ancient history now frighteningly real and at his doorstep. The goblins jeered and taunted them just beyond the range of their bows, though a few arrows had been launched in frustration.

The King limped up the stairs followed by his Chief Adviser until they too stood on the walls. "I think it would have been wise for you two to have evacuated the city with the rest of my subjects."

"What is a Chief Adviser without a king to advise, Sire?" replied Aeso.

Putting his hand on Aeso's shoulder to take the weight off his injured leg, he stared out over the vast multitude of goblins surrounding them. "I think soon there will be no King of the Elves."

Aeso's heart broke hearing the young king's words. "Do not give up hope, Sire. Is not Cassis here to help us?"

"I wish... I just wish I knew what had befallen Cassis and Loekor. I fear it will take some form of great magic or miracle to deliver us from this... this..." He trailed off, leaving the rest unsaid as he turned hobbling back down the stairs.

King Illson had barely closed his eyes when the sound of the earth rumbling and the screaming brought him quickly back to his senses.

Aeso burst into his chamber. "Lightning, lightning from the sky, Sire. It is falling down on us like rain," he blubbered.

"How can this be?" asked King Illson, quickly donning his armor. "There was not a cloud in the sky."

"There is still not a cloud to be found above, Sire." Aeso paced back and forth, his eyes darting around wildly. "What are we to do, Sire?"

"Get all the elves to cover," replied King Illson, hurrying outside. Looking up, he saw lightning bolts coming down as if thousands of spears had been thrown at once, screaming their way down to the earth. He felt hot anger rise up within him and bellowed, "face me, Dark One." Though he knew his voice carried no further than his own ears, he still hoped that maybe, just maybe, his words might still reach him.

Turning back to his palace, he paused, staring upward once more, insolence plainly showing on his face, and then he saw it. A cloud, but not an ordinary cloud. For this cloud shimmered with its own silver light as it pushed darkness before it till at last, it blanketed the Elven city. Transfixed, he stared at this shining wonder, and just as quickly as it had begun, the lightning was gone.

Outside the walls, the howls and yelps of the goblins could now be heard clearly, replacing the thunder and lightning that had only recently filled the air. The sounds of the goblins grew almost deafening, crescendoing with the cheers of the elves from the wall. Aeso hurried over to the King. "Sire, I think the miracle or great magic you had requested has arrived."

"We shall see, Aeso, we shall see."

In the hour before dawn, the King summoned what was left of his Captains. Sitting on his throne with Aeso at his side, he stared intently at the solemn faces before him. "I wish all of you to know a King could not have asked for more loyal and valiant Captains, as well as the brave elves you command." The captains, looking past him, gave him pause, and slowly turning around, his eyes grew wide, the corners of his mouth twisting upward in the beginnings of a smile. "I had wondered," he left the rest unspoken.

Lark, bloodied, his clothes in tatters, walked from behind the throne to stand with the Captains. "It was a fierce battle. Was it not?"

"Yes, yes it was," answered the King.

"We almost missed the battle; however, we were able to use the confusion of the lightning storm to slip past the goblins and into the city." He paused, taking a deep breath. "The lightning killed and maimed thousands of the enemy, but it also dealt considerable damage to my small band as well. I have lost many a good elf getting here, Sire."

"But you are here, and I am pleased that you are. However, I fear that mayhap you have walked into your own death," replied the King.

"At least it will be an honorable death, Sire."

"Come, let us partake of some fine wine during this brief respite, it may be our last," with that, the King and his entourage retired to the war room, discussing battle plans, each wondering if Cassis might not show, but one by one each dismissed this from their minds, knowing the next battle was soon to be fought.

The day dawned into a cloudless sky, the only sound being the clinking of armor as goblins made ready to assault the walls surrounding the city. The elves manning the walls looked down in disdain. The disorder of the goblins was apparent even in their great numbers. Slowly, in clinking armor, they approached those behind, pushing the ones in front ever closer.

"Now," King Illson screamed as a salvo of arrows were launched from all sides, leaving goblins squirming on the ground dead or dying. The volleys continued for hours, and still the goblins came crashing forward. Wave after wave of what seemed to be an unending tide of goblins whose numbers never seemed to decrease and whose pace never slowed.

"Sire, we are almost out of arrows, and still they come," reported a Captain.

The goblins, having reached the walls, produced crude ladders and began to scale the city walls. They hurled themselves into the waiting elvish blades, forcing them back through sheer unrelenting numbers. The fighting was fierce and bloody, the sun reflecting off the dripping gore found on most blades.

The King, with Aeso at his side, was hard-pressed on all sides by goblins. Hemmed in, hopeless of reprieve, they spied a figure cleaving and hacking its way through, kicking at the limbs and heads while wading through the gore he had created. Lark, his face and body covered in goblin blood, finally reached the King and Aeso, who were dispatching the rest of their attackers with deadly skill.

"Sire," Aeso had to yell over the din of battle. "We must make our way to the square. That is where most of us are to be found. Come, we must hurry." Turning, he decapitated a large goblin who was in the process of sneaking up on his blind side. They fought their way to the square, and it grieved the King to see how many elves had probably perished under the purple wave.

The hours of fighting were taking its toll on the elves, but even more so on any goblin who came within striking distance of the elvish blades. Seeing the battle was lost, the elves renewed their determination to take as many of the enemy with them as they could when a roar rent the air and gave pause to all but a few.

"Mayhap the Dark One has come to gloat," spat the King, to the agreement of many within range to hear him.

The roar sounded a second time, shaking the very ground they stood on. All eyes turned toward the walls, for with this second roar, a chorus of answering roars sounded from all around the city, the sound so powerful and deafening it caused buildings to collapse as if a violent earthquake had struck.

The goblins, uncertain now, milled about, fear on their faces when a crashing, equal only to thunder, came from a section of the wall as it toppled, penning and crushing several goblins below. The grackette and its riders made their way to the square, the grackette swiping and skewering goblins on the way. The goblins, so numerous, hemmed themselves in, much to the misfortune of any caught in the path of the grackette. All the goblins could think of to do was run, for nothing could withstand a grackette. Instincts instead of order ruled them now.

The goblins, retreating, scaled the walls a second time, and those who made it to the top screamed, jumping down on those waiting below. A chorus of roars, around the like of which had never been heard before, blasted through the air, and moments later, the walls cracked and buckled till the walls surrounding the city were no more. Instead, in its place stood a wall of teeth, hair, and muscle, a wall of grackette. Elves and goblins alike stood in awe of the sight, for if anyone knew anything about grackette, they knew them to be solitary animals, yet here they were. What was more amazing were the human riders of these beasts, for very, very few have ever seen a grackette and lived to tell the tale about it. There was now blind confusion as goblins darted to and fro trying to escape the gaping maws and colossal claws bearing down on them.

The first grackette to enter the city bowed down so its riders might dismount. "Sire," called Cassis. The King was so amazed at this turn of events he dropped his sword and left it laying forgotten at his feet. "How?" was all he could say. "It is Loekor who has saved this day," replied Cassis. It was then that Loekor climbed down from the beast's back and came to stand before the elves. "Sire," spoke Loekor, bowing.

"Do not bow before me, Loekor. It is I and my elves who should be honoring you." And in so saying, he bowed, followed by the elves at his side.

The noise was still deafening with the roars of the grackettes and the screams of the goblins. With Loekor's raised hand, all this ceased, and the quiet was loudest of all.

Soon, what remained of the goblins were gathered outside the city with grackettes and their human riders keeping them under guard. Even after all the fighting and the great number that fled in terror, their prisoners must have still measured within the thousands.

Surveying the carnage scattered all around him, King Illson turned, limping into the palace with slumped shoulders, feeling even though the battle was won, he had lost. Walking down the aisle to his throne, he plopped heavily down at its base. Aeso pressed a goblet of wine into his hand and stood solemnly by his side. The King gave him thanks, the sadness in his voice apparent as he looked around with hollowed eyes. "Aeso," he spoke with a tired voice, "I think the city is all but lost. There is not much left."

"We will find other lands, Sire."

"Mayhap, Aeso, mayhap."

"Sire, I know the time may not be right, but Loekor, Cassis, and Lark are waiting to see you."

"Show them in, Aeso, please."

Aeso, taken aback by the King's manner, thought it best to hold his tongue as he went to fetch them.

Loekor, leading the small procession, took note of the King's dejected expression, the nonchalant way he sat on the throne. "Sire," he spoke, bowing down.

"There is no reason to be formal, Loekor. Without your help, I would not be sitting here today."

"Sire," intoned Loekor, "Without your brave leadership, there would have been nothing for us to come back to."

"Mayhap, Loekor," shaking himself out of his reverie, he stared at Loekor as if seeing him for the first time. "What has happened to you, my friend?" he asked, seeing the way Loekor's antlers glowed, the shimmering robe of many colors, and ornate scepter. There could be no doubt it was the Scepter of Soren, the power emanating from it almost palpable. The biggest change the King saw was in Loekor himself, his bearing as he stood before him. Loekor related all the events that had transpired on their way to Mount Kan and their trip back.

"It is a strange tale, and it was you who protected us from the lightning bolts?"

"Yes, Sire, with Cassis and Maloc's help in directing me. I wish I could have done more, but the power of the scepter is limited, and I have yet to master its forces."

"I wish I had been as successful as you, my friend. I consider all of you friends and allies, so it is with a heavy heart I tell you this. I feel as though I've failed as a ruler. I've let my kingdom all but perish."

It was then Cassis stepped forward, with Lark close in her footsteps. "King Illson, it is true many brave elves died here today, but it is also true many good elves lived thanks to the leadership of you and your captains. When we reached the Plains of Leon, we thought all of you had perished, the bodies as numerous as the blades of grass."

"We will rebuild," interrupted Lark. "We will build the greatest Elvish city that has ever existed. A monument to those that have fallen in battle."

The King looked as if a great burden had been lifted from his shoulders. "We, Lark?" he asked.

"Yes, Sire, we. That is if you will allow me to serve you."

Stepping down, the King embraced Lark. "For the goblins' part in this," spoke Loekor, "they shall help rebuild, for better stone cutters are not to be found."

"Why should they be spared?" asked Lark.

"Though they are a vile race unto themselves, it was the Dark One's influence which led them to battle this time. Without the Dark One to lead them, I think they will find other things to while away their time."

Cassis excused herself to see if she might find the goblin who claimed to be the ambassador of peace, if he still lived. She found not only had he lived but that he had come through the battle without so much as a scratch. With the goblin in tow, as well as the black-haired giant who had first taken up arms for Loekor, they proceeded to the palace.

The goblin, sure of his doom, shuffled slowly forward with Cassis and the black-haired man on either side of him. Looking up at the King with his large, lidless eyes, an audible gulp escaped him. "Sire," he croaked.

"I have been advised to spare your life, ambassador."

A shudder shook the short, squat form. "Do you find that agreeable?"

"Yes, Sire! Thank you, Sire!" squeaked the goblin, not quite believing his good fortune.

"There will be a price for this."

"Anything, Sire, anything." Relief washed over the goblin, more sure of his footing now.

"You and your allies have seen fit to help destroy my city. I hope you will be inclined to help rebuild it. For this, I will spare your life as well as your fellow goblins." The King gave the goblin a scowling look as he looked down on the quaking figure. "And if ever you or yours raise arms against us again, we will not be so forgiving."

"But Sire, if we do this for you, then the Dark One will have vengeance on us."

Loekor stepped forward. "Do not be afraid of the Dark One, for shortly I believe he will be very preoccupied. The King has seen fit to give you a second chance. You would be well advised to take it and lead your race out from under the Dark One's power."

The bargain was struck, and the goblin was returned to his own. Shortly thereafter, all were in agreement to help the elves rebuild. It was a small price for life and freedom.

Two days later, Loekor and Cassis bid the elves goodbye with a promise to return. The coming battle would be between Loekor and the Dark One, a battle of power. A battle between light and darkness.

"It seems strange, Cassis."

"What is that, Loekor?"

"Not to have Therseus with us."

"Yes, Loekor, it does seem strange," replied Cassis, a catch in her voice as a tear traced its way down her craggy face. "I miss him too." The two sat in silence for a moment until Cassis, changing the subject, broke the silence. "It was wise of you to suggest the goblins help the elves rebuild. The King will grieve less for his elves while he's building for the future."

"That was part of my thinking, but it is good to know the goblins will be kept busy and hopefully not interfering with what we must do. The grackette's will return back to the wilds within a couple of days, but I think the people will stay with the elves for a while longer."

"Do you suppose the elves will find that which they have lost?" Cassis replied.

Loekor stopped and looked down at Cassis. "Yes, now that the elves are united once more, I believe that they will. With Lark's and Aeso's guidance, I believe that the King will create a kingdom great enough to surpass even that of his father."

CHAPTER TWENTY
Breaking the Spell

A day's travel behind them, Loekor judged the many miles they had covered. It was made easier with Cassis assuming her cloud shape to better escalate their speed. She knew she would never be able to keep up with Loekor in her regular form.

As they stopped to make camp, the moon hung high in the sky, casting an eerie glow over the bleak landscape. The large rocks, illuminated by the lunar light, gleamed white as bone. The sparsely-leaved trees seemed to twist and writhe in agony, their bare branches reaching up to the unforgiving moon as if beseeching it for mercy.

Loekor could feel the eyes of predators on them and sometimes hear the ferocious fighting of large animals, but never did they venture into the small circle of light cast by the small fire. It was just as well, for Cassis had produced another of her numerous pouches and sprinkled its powder in a protective circle. Loekor listened to the last of her incantation, and even though he knew Cassis's spells were strong, he gripped the scepter even harder, hearing the death throes of one of the numerous animals circling their camp.

Topping a small mountain range the next morning, they stared at the land they would have to cross.

"I have never seen a land like this," said Loekor. "It's as though it is dead."

"Do not be deceived, Loekor." Looking out over the desert, Cassis perceived numerous small dust devils traversing in their spiral courses across the dry land. "We should be on the other side before nightfall finds us again."

As the day wore on, Loekor and Cassis grew more apprehensive, the feeling of something stalking them becoming almost unbearable. Tiring, the sun sapping their strength, they made their way to an outcropping of rocks and sat under its meager shade. They watched the heat rising from the arid desert floor.

"I do not like this place," repeated Loekor, sipping from a waterskin the elves had provided. Even though the waterskin was small, it seemed the water was always abundant, never seeming to diminish. "I wish I knew more of the power of the scepter."

"I've taught you all I know of the Scepter. As for the rest, it will come when the time is right." Accepting the waterskin from Loekor, she drank deeply, closing her eyes and enjoying the cool water as it wet her parched throat.

"I'm still not sure, Cassis. I fear I will never be the wizard Soren was."

"Put these doubts aside, Loekor. It was written before time that you would be the possessor of the scepter. It will be you who will dispel this evil once and for all."

"Could you not cast a spell to mayhap see what our enemy might be doing?" Loekor inquired.

"I wish I could, Loekor, but the Dark One has prevented this. Even with Maloc's help, I was not able to get past his weave of power."

"Cassis, does it not concern you that he has not tried to stop us?"

"We are not there yet. I'm sure he knows you have the scepter. Perhaps he is waiting to see if you have mastered the scepter and its power before he moves against us. After all, you did stop the goblin army he loosed."

"Do not forget our brave allies, Cassis."

"The brave elves who fell in battle will never be forgotten. Of that, you can be sure. Mayhap when this is over, we will have time to grieve for all those brave warriors who have perished, like Therseus."

"Yes, like Therseus," repeated Loekor, bowing his head. Enjoying the shade under the rocks, they stretched out and were soon asleep.

A tingling followed by a throbbing in his hand brought Loekor out of his deep sleep. "Cassis, Cassis, wake up!"

Reluctantly, she did so. "What happened?" she asked, stretching and yawning.

"We fell asleep, I'm afraid. Something is not right," he said, surveying the surrounding country and not discerning anything unusual. "I believe it was the scepter that woke me."

"There is danger then," said Cassis, shaking off the last of her grogginess. "I believe we were under some sort of spell."

It was then they noticed the shadows cast by the rock move, dissecting themselves from the larger shadow. Soon it was as if a cloud hid the sun's light, with the shadows blanketing the ground.

"Who dares enter this land unbidden," spoke a large shadow floating across the ground until it was a scant two feet from Loekor. "All who come here must die for this trespass."

"We mean you no harm, whoever you are," said Loekor, holding the scepter protectively in front of him. "We just wish to cross your lands on our quest. We take nothing from it. If we trespass, we are sorry."

"It is too late," said the shadow, now floating off the ground until it seemed to be standing on translucent legs.

Cassis and Loekor backed further into the lee of the rock.

"What sort of beings are these?" whispered Loekor.

"I'm not sure. I've heard stories, but these were few and incomplete, and I'm starting to see why."

Stepping forward, Loekor asked, "Who be you shadows?"

"Since your lives are forfeit, I will tell you," spoke the shadow, gliding closer to Loekor. "Once this land was bountiful, not barren as you see it now. I was king and ruler of this land. We were called Messianites, a proud race, mayhap too proud. As it was, a stranger came into our land, a wizard. No stranger than yourself," said the shadow, circling Loekor. "You are seeing his spell even now as we speak."

"I don't—"

"Silence, horned one," the shadow stood in front of him once more. "I had a daughter. A more beautiful princess could not be had. The wizard approached me for her hand in marriage. For this, I had him thrown into the dungeon. As I said, mayhap too proud. After a year, I released him and thought him gone. As it was, he hid in the hills. I paid him no more heed, even though I heard rumors of a wild man living in the hills. He was building his power, of this, I'm sure, but now it is of no matter."

Cassis interrupted, "You say all of this," spreading her arms, she encompassed the desert, "is a wizard's spell?"

"Yes," answered the shadow, moving even closer, its interest in these two strangers growing more aroused. "Why do you ask?"

"If a wizard casts a spell, it's possible another may break it."

"Do not jest with me, aged one." The shadow grew a darker shade and it's voice grew more menacing.

"I do not jest," said Cassis. "There is only one who could cast a spell like the one befallen to you, but letting you throw him into your dungeon, that I do not understand. Unless his power was very weak or perhaps drained. Tell me, did this spell also include bad manners?"

"You talk brave, considering your destiny."

"We will try to help you if you promise to let us, and other travelers henceforth, cross your lands in peace and safety."

"And if this does not work?"

"We shall see," answered Cassis.

The shadow seemed to stiffen but kept silent. Cassis turned to Loekor. "It is up to you now."

Loekor removed his cloak and agilely scaled the rock outcropping. Upon reaching the top, he sat down, crossing his legs, the scepter gripped tightly in a sweaty hand.

"You can do it," Cassis called from below.

Loekor closed his eyes, feeling the hot desert breeze on his skin. His ears picked up the faint sighing of the furnace-blasted wind. After a few minutes, he felt the power building, starting at his hooves, lancing up his legs, encompassing his upper body, the feeling almost painful as the power integrated itself with him. Gripping the scepter even tighter, the knuckles of his hand turning white, he almost screamed when a silence enveloped him, caressing him in its embrace. Then it was as a window being opened, and looking out of this, Loekor saw the land as it had been. A rushing river with large trees bordering its sides, and small farms cut in perfect squares. Dominating all of this stood a castle built of rough stone. A pleasant place, he thought, staring upwards and almost losing his concentration. Seeing the web covering the sky, its green filaments stretching away further than his eyes could see. It resembles a spider's web, he thought to himself. Coming out of his trance, he beckoned Cassis to him and related all that he had seen.

After hearing all that Loekor described, Cassis squatted, drawing runes on the hard-packed earth. "I think we can help them, Loekor," she said, getting up. "But it will take both of our magics." She reached into her robe, extracting a foul-smelling powder, and handed it to Loekor while explaining what they had to do.

Locating a higher peak, Loekor threw the powder in the four directions Cassis had indicated. The powder was supposed to cut the four largest threads anchoring the web to the ground, while she intoned an incantation to help guide and strengthen the powder. With this done, Loekor held the scepter aloft, twirling it faster than the eye could see. Soon, a shaft of light appeared from the scepter, arcing into the sky, spreading its glow until the web was illuminated for all to see. Ceasing his twirling, he grasped the scepter by its end, swinging it around his head, the yellow shaft of light still attached. In a few moments, a maelstrom was created, the wind shrieking overhead as the web wrapped around and around itself until it was nothing but a ball of yellow sun, easily fitting into the palm of Loekor's hand. He handed it to Cassis, who placed it in an empty pouch and quickly secreted it into her robe. The winds shrieking overhead grew even louder as the desert floor undulated. The motion caused large boulders to roll back and forth across its surface. Loekor lowered his scepter, and instantly a silence ensued as all motion ceased.

"Now, Loekor!" Cassis screamed.

Hearing this, Loekor pointed the scepter downward, and a hissing crevice appeared. Spying the crevice, Cassis approached its edge. Withdrawing the leather pouch holding the miniature sun, she threw it into the scalding crack of earth.

Soon, thousands of tiny cracks appeared, several spewing water upward while others sprouted trees from their dark enclosures. With a loud rumbling, the earth turned over into itself, and green pastures grew where once only desert stood. In other places, the ground grew skyward to form mountains, some with waterfalls cascading downward to form a large lake with a river passing through it.

Houses sprung up where once was only dirt. A tremendous shaking grasped the ground once more, and a castle appeared, stone by stone, its spires stabbing at the sky, at last completed.

"Now for the last," said Cassis.

"Yes, yes it is," replied Loekor, while tears streamed down his face in joy at what they had undone. "And it is also good to have a witch as an ally and friend," Loekor's voice choked out.

Cassis reached up, grasping Loekor's hand, squeezing it as she smiled up into his face, tears threatening her own eyes. Still holding his hand, they waited for the King, who was fast approaching, a large smile shining out from between his beard and mustache.

CHAPTER TWENTY-ONE
Waking in Darkness

Therseus woke in the night disoriented, the pain in his shoulder and leg a dull throbbing. Trying to sit up, he winced, his shoulder feeling as if a hot brand had been put there. His eyes watered while he gasped for breath. Falling back, he almost passed out, but willed himself back from the brink.

Running his tongue over cracked lips, he tried to swallow but found this all but impossible. Then he remembered the night, the lightning, the goblins, and he choked back a sob.

A stirring to his left gave him cause to look in that direction, but all he could discern was a shadow moving towards him. Unconsciously, he reached for his skinning knife before remembering he had discarded it with his clothes in the elvish kingdom when he changed into the clothes of the Dark Elves. Closing his eyes to mere slits, he waited.

The shadow loomed directly overhead, bending down. Now! His brain screamed, but his arm refused to move.

"You are awake, that is good," a soft voice said. "I was afraid you would never wake."

"Theena is that you?" Therseus croaked, his throat hurting with the effort.

"Yes, Therseus, it is I."

"What of the other?"

"I fear—I fear we are the only ones left." Gently, she probed his shoulder and then his leg. "I was not sure our herbs would work on mort— on you."

"I feel very weak."

"You lost a lot of blood. Do you think you might be able to eat?" Rising, she crossed the small cave, coming back with a small wooden bowl.

The mention of food caused an involuntary grumble to issue from his stomach.

Theena held the bowl to his lips. Therseus noisily gulped the hot broth, relishing its taste and finishing it quickly.

"Thank you," he smiled weakly, "I did not realize how hungry I was. How, how long has it been?"

"Five days and four nights have passed," she replied.

"We must," Therseus started to say but grunting with the pain, he fell back, the effort too much for him.

"You must rest, Therseus." Gently, she laid a hand on his forehead, brushing the hair from his sweaty face.

Therseus tried to fight to stay awake, but this was one battle he lost, feeling himself slip back into the dark void of sleep.

CHAPTER TWENTY-TWO

Trapped in the Cavern of the Tiny Warriors

"I think our Messianite guide might have been right about this place. What forest is this, Cassis?" asked Loekor.

"I do not know, but it is a dismal and dreary place," responded Cassis, looking into its dark depths. The trees were almost black in color and dressed in dark green moss. Drawing a breath of the dank, almost suffocating air, she gagged at the stench of dead vegetation strong in her nostrils.

"It is strange the way the moss clings to every inch of the trees like a thick blanket. Look, it even grows from treetop to treetop."

An involuntary shiver shook Cassis' small frame, but not from the cold, for the air felt tropical. "The Dark One picks strange paths to follow."

The Messianite who had guided them to the edge of the gloomy forest had long since turned back. Wishing them good luck, he had left them not daring to set foot in this, what he called an evil place. They followed the weak but persistent light that the staff's orb gave off.

"I fear we will not pass through this place before nightfall catches us," said Loekor. He felt his hooves sink into the mushy carpet of decay, a sucking noise ensuing when he withdrew his hoof for the next step.

They had stopped to rest, but very few minutes had passed before the moss dropped from the treetops in sticky strands to slowly try to cover them. Amazed and repulsed, Loekor and Cassis trudged on, the wet heat taking its toll. Cassis had tried to take her cloud form earlier, but the air itself had prevented this, not allowing her to rise.

As they entered deeper into the forest, a chorus of high-pitched chirps pierced their ears, growing louder and more frantic. It grew in intensity until it was unbearable. Cassis clasped her hands over her ears, but found this didn't help the noise entering her very being. Looking towards Loekor, she was distressed at seeing him on his knees, large clumps of moss covering his upper body.

"Loekor," she screamed, trying to make her way to him even as moss covered her.

"Cassis," he choked out, "I can't move. Run while you have the chance."

"I – I don't think that's possible," she rasped, tearing at the moss to no avail.

"The scepter is out of my hands. I can't reach it. The moss, it's alive. It's preventing me from getting it back," he groaned with the effort completely covered except for his head.

As they lay there entombed, the moss spewed a sickly yellow cloud to cover the forest floor and its two hapless victims. Cassis and Loekor in their struggles unwittingly breathed in the gas; its cloying odor overtaking them, and in seconds, it carried their consciousness far away.

Feebly opening his heavy eyelids, his mind still sluggish from the effects of the gas, Loekor tried to stretch his overly tired limbs but found this impossible. Reality slowly coming back, he tried desperately to break loose from his bonds, struggling in vain. "Cassis," he whispered.

"Here, Loekor, over here," Cassis called out.

Straining, he managed to turn his head and spied her in a corner, trussed as he was in heavy vines.

"Where—" he began to ask.

Anticipating his question, she answered, "In the other corner, over there."

He saw the scepter leaning against the rock wall next to their packs, impossible to reach. Dragging his eyes away, he stared at their surroundings, seeing the dim orange glow that cast eerie shadows on the cave walls came from clumps of moss adhering to the small caverns walls.

"Where are we?" he asked, his whispered voice echoing back to him.

"I do not know, Loekor. All I remember was the moss and then...eyes?" Her voice trailed off.

"Cassis, Cassis, what is it?" Loekor's anguished voice asked. Then he heard it too, a chirping, and what sounded like the stamping of many tiny feet slowly approaching.

Turning his head in the direction the sound came from, he was astonished at the small creatures standing next to his face, studying him. Barely four inches tall and insect in appearance, all but the head egg-shaped but not much different than his own except for the antenna waving angrily in the air. The light from the moss reflected off their shells as they danced around on four legs. In their two hands, most held tiny spears and ornate shields which also reflected the light, their tiny reflections dotting Loekor's face.

One of the creature's stepped closer than the rest, jabbing his spear into the side of Loekor's face, a tiny trickle of blood following.

"Ouch," Loekor mouthed, the spear point feeling like a pinprick. He redoubled his efforts at breaking the bonds, but they still held fast.

The chirping grew louder than before. Loekor looked again at the small oddities and witnessed his tiny assailant being dragged back. It seemed to Loekor the small beings were arguing amid angry arm-waving. After a few minutes of this, they appeared to come to some concession before they turned and marched off. The moss that had been hiding the entrance lifted up and permitted their exit.

"Cassis, did you see them?" Loekor asked, turning towards her.

"Yes, I did, but what they are I cannot say," replied Cassis.

"Perhaps the Dark One's minions?"

"I think not. If they were, surely this scepter would be in the Dark One's hands." Straining, she managed a sitting position. "If I could just reach inside my robe." Trying, it was all she could do just to move her fingers. "I never would have thought something so small would stop us on our quest."

Blinking and squeezing his eyes shut, he readjusted them to the dim light, wishing he could reach their packs and water. The gas having left a sweetish sour taste in his mouth.

"Do not give up, Loekor. It's not over yet," she said, though she wished her own thoughts weren't of resignation to how hopelessly they were trapped.

It seemed like days had passed before they returned. This time, they were led by one half the size as the rest and sporting transparent wings. Approaching Cassis, the small creature scrutinized her, then reached out, touching her withered skin.

"I know you," it chirped. "From stories." Folding its four legs, it squatted in front of her. "You are Cassis," it spoke. "You are the witch of the Blue Forest."

"Yes, I am Cassis," she replied, astonished. She searched her memory for some clue, any clue that would help her identify this strange race, but nothing came forth.

"Have you come to battle the evil corrupting our lands?"

"Yes, I have," she replied, hoping it was the right answer.

"You have come far, very far from your homeland." Clapping his hands, the smaller creatures clambered over her, cutting at the vines till at last she was free, her circulation returning painfully. "You must forgive us our caution, for these are troubled times and we take no chances." Chirping and pointing at Loekor, the tiny creatures advanced on him, and very soon he was also free.

"It was giants such as you that came in the name of the Dark One and waged war on us. We were all but defeated till we befriended the moss."

"Who may you be?" Cassis asked while rubbing the stiffness from her arms and legs.

"My name is Zeeratte. We are of the tribe Geesing." Zeeratte noticed the way Loekor's eye strayed to the packs. "Before we talk, refresh yourselves."

Thanking him, Loekor got up, wincing with the sharp stinging pains in his legs. Careful not to step on the tiny Geesings, he retrieved their packs and the scepter. Sated, he and Cassis relayed their tales and travels to Zeeratte, who in turn relayed it to his people in a high chirping noise. Zeeratte was an apt listener, asking questions now and then.

"I myself am a wizard," Zeeratte said. "I tried to battle this evil you speak of and I am ashamed to say I was no match for this evil being. I retreated here, my home, and almost brought destruction to my race. I guess he thought us not worth the effort and soon he left but not before sealing the entrance to our true domain."

"Where is your true domain?" Loekor asked, caught up in the

small wizard's story.

"Ah, Horned one. It is a cavern of wondrous beauty and light. Fresh cold spring water forming a lake, trees, and fruits to satisfy our every need. Alas, it is lost. I have tried to remove the spell that blocks it, but even so, the boulder behind the spell is much too large for us to move from the entrance." Zeeratte seemed to shrink into his shell, his head hanging downward in dejection.

Loekor, if possible, would have laid a comforting hand on Zeeratte's shoulder. "Come, Zeeratte, and show Cassis and me this special place. Perhaps it's possible not all is lost."

Zeeratte looked up and asked, "You mean you will help us even after the way you were treated?" Loekor replied, "It is as you say, a dangerous time, a time for caution." Cassis nodded in agreement. With that, Zeeratte turned to his people and explained to them in their own language, and upon hearing what had transpired, they beat their shields with their spears in thanks and hearty approval.

Stepping out into the gloom of day, the strange party of two giants and a small Geesing struck out west. In just a little over an hour's travel, they brought them to the boulder. "It is just a boulder," said Loekor, reaching out to feel its rough-textured surface. On contact with his hand, he felt a jolt shoot up his arm, numbing it as he was knocked away. He could easily understand the danger to the tiny Geesings. Backing a little further away, he took a wide-legged stance, the scepter in front of him, gripped in both hands.

Cassis came to stand beside Loekor. "Will you be able to break the spell?"

"I think so. It does not seem to be very powerful. Besides, it is time to see if your pupil has learned." He took a brief moment to smile down on Cassis.

Cassis was quick to notice that Loekor showed a confidence he had not exuded before. "I think our wizard is born, Soren," she thought to herself.

Loekor continued his concentration, feeling the power build, tingling, lifting. Gasping, he felt it travel down his arm through his finger and finally into the scepter itself. The Geesings felt the magic in the air, their antennas waving uncertainly, searching. As the orb adorning the scepter grew bright and brighter, they retreated out of sight, all except Zeeratte, who, with Cassis, had backed away a few paces.

The orb continued to brighten, its white light blinding. It lit the forest in its ethereal glow, the trees casting grotesque shadows in its wake. Cassis and Zeeratte covered their eyes, their ears hearing a high-pitched hum coming from the direction of Loekor, their feet feeling a vibration coming from the very ground itself.

Loekor released the power, sending it arcing into the boulder. At first, the boulder seemed untouched by this intrusion. "What—" Zeeratte clamped his mouth shut, watching the pulsing white veins of light covering the boulder. It seemed to him the veins melted into the boulder, leaving it fractured in many places. As he watched, Loekor swung the scepter, stopping it as it came in line with the center of the boulder. The explosion of power lifted him, throwing him back. Rising to his knees, he saw the entrance to the cavern before him.

"Are you alright?" asked Cassis, bending down and helping Zeeratte to stand.

"Yes, I think so," he answered, his four legs still wobbly. "He is a powerful wizard."

"Yes, he is a powerful wizard," Cassis intoned.

"It is a good thing the moss knocked him out," Zeeratte thought to himself. "If he would have had the chance to cast a spell—" He admonished himself for this train of thought. "Did he not befriend us?"

Warily, the Geesings came out of hiding in twos and threes until they were all gathered around Zeeratte.

"Loekor, Cassis," spoke up Zeeratte. "My tribe and myself thank you for this great boon you have done us." Saying this, he bowed down on two legs, the other Geesings quickly following his example.

Rising, he hurried to the cavern's entrance, beckoning Loekor and Cassis to follow him. Loekor and Cassis slowly approached the mouth and stepped in, Loekor having to duck his head.

As they stood in the threshold, they stared with wonder at the beauty spread out before them. Their eyes traveled upwards, seeing the crystal covering the roof of the cavern radiating a light to equal the very sun itself.

The light from the crystal cast a perpetual rainbow over the bluest of lakes, its waves gently lapping the white sandy shores. Small trees of the like they had never seen bore a variety of fruits of every description and color that stretched away as far as the eye could see.

They stood awestruck at the size of the cavern, seeing why this would indeed seem like the whole world to the Geesings, which it was.

As night approached, the Geesings changed; their shells sparked, then coming aglow, resembling a lightning bug on a warm summer's night.

"Look, Cassis," said Loekor, pointing at the Geesings, "they have changed." He sat back, enjoying the night, nibbling on a piece of the fruit found so numerous on the trees. "They are a beautiful race."

"Yes, they are," agreed Cassis. She figured the metamorphosis had something to do with the crystal, its lights dancing high overhead.

They stayed with the Geesings that night, vowing they would resume their quest on the morrow.

Before they left, Zeeratte presented them with small carved whistles. "For your help, we have adopted you and Cassis into our tribe. If ever either of you should need our help, just blow on the whistles, and remember, you are always welcomed here in our world. Do not fear the moss; you will pass in safety."

Starting out in the direction Zeeratte had showed them, Loekor stopped, turned, and waved before he and Cassis disappeared into the trees. They traveled all that day and night without mishap, to their relief, emerging from dark trees bordering the even darker forest.

They had grown used to the close confines of the trees, so the panoramic view before them had a quieting effect on them, an unnerving feeling of being watched. Loekor bent, retrieving several large pieces of deadwood, assuming wood might be hard to find on the treeless expanse before them.

Looking to each other one more time, they stepped out from the sanctuary of the trees. Cassis embodied her cloud form once more, drifting inches above the short grass, easily pacing Loekor.

They traveled half that day before stopping to rest, making a noon meal out of the fruit Zeeratte had sent with them.

"I feel exposed, Cassis. I know it sounds feeble, but the feeling of being watched closely stays with me."

"I know, Loekor. The feeling is the same for me."

"Have you noticed there is not one sign of life, not even the droning of an insect?"

He had no sooner said this when the ground shifted below them, a bowl-shaped indentation taking form.

"Watch out," Loekor hollered, taking Cassis's hand and quickly pulling her out of the bottom of the circle of dirt, the bottom undulating and growing deeper.

"What happened?" he asked, standing on shaky legs.

In answer, a scaled arm shot out of the hole as thick as Loekor's waist. Waving in the air, it resembled an entranced cobra in its movements. Stretching, it soared another ten feet into the air, its tip twisting and searching. Now as tall as the trees they had only recently left behind, the beast turned its bottom side, looking like that of an octopus, but where the suction cups would have been, there were a series of hooks, and from these dripped a purple-colored liquid hissing and searing the ground as it rained down.

In his hurry to get away, Loekor grasped Cassis, placing her under his arm, and ran for his life, putting great distance between them and the beast in a very short time. Feeling it was safe, he stopped, gasping for breath, and set Cassis gently down.

Cassis, indignant at being carried like a frightened child, held her tongue, knowing Loekor just wanted to get them away from danger.

On wobbly legs, Loekor all but fell on the short grass, his chest heaving. "It is no wonder animals do not graze this place," he choked out, chuckling. He turned this into a boisterous laugh, trying to replace the terror he really felt. "I never would have even dreamed of the creatures and oddities we have come across on this quest." He laid the scepter across his folded legs, laying his palms flat on the ground, ready to bolt at the slightest of tremors.

"Our quest is far from over," said Cassis.

Loekor meditated on this while catching his breath.

CHAPTER TWENTY-THREE
The Demon's Flight

"So, you have escaped my pet," snickered the dark cloaked figure, his long, tapered fingers drumming nonchalantly on the thigh bones forming the arms of what he liked to think of as his throne. Airily waving his right hand, the silver sphere on the wall shrunk, the figures within diminishing. "They should be more cautious," he said more to himself than to the harpy perched on a low ledge, its talons gouging holes in the hard rock surface. He rose, pacing the cave, a hellish red light shining out from the hood covering his head. Balling a fist, he slammed it into the open palm of his other hand, the loud report causing dust to drift down from the cave's roof.

The harpy hunkered down, hiding its head under a wing. It feared its master in his rage.

He stopped his pacing to stand in front of the winged apparition. "Do not be scared, my foul-feathered pet." The harpy slowly raised its head from under its wing. Reaching out, he stroked its filthy head. "Only those who have betrayed me shall die." He giggled at this as if it were his own private joke. He thought of the goblins and the pleasure he would derive from their suffering. "It shall be soon, my feathered one, it shall be soon."

He returned to his grisly throne, hesitating, a decision weighing heavily on him. "My power quickly evaporates," he thought to himself. "I need the scepter. Surely they are close enough." Decided, he walked over to the small pool etched into the rock's hard surface. Looking into its green, bubbling depths, he spied several dark objects swimming to and from, waiting.

Reaching into the pool, he extracted one of the dark, wiggly shapes. It resembled a black grub worm in appearance. Stepping away from the pool, he laid the squirming object gently on the rock floor. Cooing to it, he stripped off his cape, covering it with this. Squatting on his heels, he chanted a chant that even the oldest of the wizards and witches had long forgotten.

The harpy squawked, afraid, seeing the form beneath the cape take shape, growing till its head all but touched the ceiling. The black cape barely covered the head and part of the shoulders, the tips of wings even now unfolding, flexing, the cave not wide enough to accommodate them. A loud hissing escaped from beneath the cape, followed by a putrid stench filling the cave in nauseating waves.

The Dark One casually approached the abomination, reaching out, jerking the cape back to expose the hideous head. The creature now freed hissed and gurgled, slobbering, the yellow sulfurous drops scarring the floor, bubbling into black pools.

Seeing the Dark One, it laid back its large fowl-like ears, opening its elongated mouth, brandishing its two dagger-like fangs crowning its wicked-looking teeth. "Oh yes, yes, my pet," laughed the Dark One, his evil laugh matching the merciless eyes staring at him, red slitted eyes devoid of pupils. "You will do nicely," he crooned. Reaching out, he felt the velvety black wings, caressing them. He led the demon to the mouth of the cave, its crawling resembling that of a bat. "Bring me the Scepter of Soren," he whispered into its ear.

The demon stood, stretching its impossibly long arms to thirty feet, the leathery skin attached to these billowing in the slight breeze. The large red veins mapping the wings seemed to pulse with a life of their own. Slowly, lazily, the wings beat the air, and with a loud hissing, the demon launched itself into the welcoming blackness, the night winds carrying the creature aloft. The dark sky hid its passing as if ashamed it had borne him. As it flew, the demon flexed its hands, curling its eight razor-sharp talons found on each hand, anxious, scenting, hunting its quarry.

CHAPTER TWENTY-FOUR

A Demon in the Cabin

"There it is again, look," Loekor pointed. The pinpoint of light abruptly winked out, just as it had done for the past thirty minutes.

"There is only one way to find out," said Cassis, sliding down the steep bank. The sandy bottom muffled her descent. Loekor joined her, and as they did, they stealthily made their way to the crude wooden cabin, the darkness helping them cover their approach. Finding the doorway, minus the door, they waited on either side, their backs pressed against the cool moss adhering to the rough out logs. It seemed hours had passed before Cassis nodded, and seeing her signal, Loekor stepped into the blackness, the scepter casting a dim bluish light on the cabin's meager furnishing. A crude table with two chairs and shelves held the weight of many earthen jugs. One wall was covered with cupboards from the floor to the ceiling, most of these with crude locks.

"It is empty," making his way back to the doorway, he was almost there when the trap-door swung open, sending him sprawling on the sandy dirt floor.

"Loekor— Loekor, what is it?" Cassis hissed, her harsh whisper cutting through the stillness.

"I think I was attacked," replied Loekor, rubbing his bruised leg. "I saw a flash of light and then found myself on the floor." Loekor saw a small dark shadow entering the doorway. "Over here," he whispered.

Squatting down, Cassis gingerly felt Loekor's leg. "I do not feel anything broken but—," the trap-door swung out again, the light from within forming a halo around the small figure, his mumbled curses bitten off. Surprise showed on his face as he slammed the door shut. "Go away, away, I say. I've done everything asked of me." The voice was deep and sonorous.

"And what is it that you did?" Cassis asked.

"Did I not help your army!" the muffled voice replied.

Even though Cassis had caught the barest of glances, she knew what it was they faced. Placing her hand on Loekor's shoulder, she bade him stay as she picked her way over to the concealed door. "Come out."

A tone of suspicion crept into the voice, "Who are you?" Before he received an answer, he all but screamed, "No, you have no right, no right at all. Go away," the deep shaky voice repeated.

"I, Cassis, Witch of the Blue Forest, demand you come out or suffer my wrath." The minutes passed in silence, the only noise being from Loekor as he crawled over to Cassis.

"What is it?" Loekor asked, his whispered voice thundering in the small confines of the doorless cabin.

"It is a gnome."

"What is a gnome?"

"It is a creature who puts more store in treasure above anything else, even above friends." Cassis no longer whispering, hoping this would evoke a response, which was shortly forthcoming.

"That is a dirty lie!" the muffled voice responded. "It is a filthy lie, and may a grackette scatter your cleaned bones upon the land."

"Brave talk for one that hides underground, shaking like the rest of his breed," mumbled cursing sounded from under them before the voice rang out. "Leave, leave my dwelling. You were not invited here, you are not wanted here."

Loekor leaned forward, whispering to Cassis, "Maybe we should leave."

"We need information, and he can provide that, but we must keep him talking till we can get him out, or else he may tunnel away," she whispered back. "We'll drag you from your hole," Cassis said to the gnome, her voice very calm. "Or I shall cast a spell and blow you out of your miserable little hole."

"Beware, the goblins found here do not take kindly to strangers in their lands. They'll place you on a spit and cook you well done," threatened the gnome.

"So," Cassis's voice took on a sinister sound, "you are an ally and friend to the goblins."

"I did not say that!" the muffled voice replied.

"I have no time for foolish games. Come out now!" she said, her voice growing louder, her patience lost.

"No."

Cassis, with temper flaring and with grinding teeth, reached inside her robe, withdrawing a pouch. "You asked for it."

Loekor placed a hand on her shoulder in hopes of restraining her and held up his other for silence. "Wait," he whispered, straddling the concealed door. Feeling under the sand, he found the rough wooden edges he sought. Drawing in a deep breath, he pulled, the wood groaning under the onslaught. One more heave, and the door came loose, the splintered wood answering defeat as Loekor lost his balance, tumbling across the floor. The door still grasped tightly in his hands, the frightened gnome attached to the opposing side.

Gaining his feet, the gnome screamed obscenities, flailing blindly at his captor, who easily held him off with one arm.

"Hold him, Loekor," Cassis said, finding and lighting an oil lamp.

The gnome, seeing Loekor cast in the meager glow of the lamp, grunted his surprise, his eyes widening, and resumed his attack with renewed vigor until Loekor reached down, plucking him easily from the floor. The gnome continued his kicking, curses spilling from his mouth.

"What do I do with him?" Loekor asked, barely avoiding the teeth snapping at his arm.

"Bind him," said Cassis, "and bind his foul mouth as well." She added as almost an afterthought. She watched the struggling gnome with no small amount of amusement.

Loekor accomplished this, but not without getting bitten and kicked several times.

The squirming gnome's hostile eyes never wavered from Cassis and Loekor as he tried to free his hands with no success. "Aul et ou," he mumbled through the gag, sure that these two strangers were here to rob him.

"Do you think he sides with the Dark One?" Loekor asked, nodding toward their captive and seeing the little gnome's face was almost as red as the hair found on his head, matching the red beard stretching from his face to end at overly large feet.

"Mayhap it's possible," she replied while rummaging in the shelves found closest to the doorway. "When our friend cools down a bit, we shall ask him." She was well aware of a gnome's temper and their devious nature.

After making a meal out of what stores she had found, she and Loekor enjoyed the simple fare. The food finished, she beckoned Loekor to remove the now-soaked gag, wondering how many curse words might be trapped in the rag.

"Before you speak, gnome, this is for the food." Reaching into her robe, she brought forth a single chunk of gold, and this she threw at the gnome's foot. "I'm sure you will find that sufficient." She noticed the greed surfacing on the gnome's face, the bulbous nose growing redder, the scent of gold strong in his nostrils.

"I think you can release him now, Loekor, and mayhap who knows, maybe he will be a little more considerate towards his guests."

Upon his release, the gnome scrambled after the chunk of metal, placing it in his mouth, testing. "It is real," he said to himself, clapping his hands in glee. "Gold, yes gold, and more gold." He danced a little jig to Loekor's astonishment. Seeming to just notice Loekor and Cassis, he closed a grimy hand on the gold, his smile as innocent as that of a child.

"Well," he said with a purring voice, "why did you not just say you were willing to pay your way?"

Loekor uneasily squatted down beside Cassis, all the while keeping a close eye on the gnome, still not quite believing the transformation which had taken place. "There must be great magic in that rock," he whispered to Cassis.

The gnome disappeared into the hole that had been hidden by the trap door but not before calling over his shoulder, "make yourselves at home. I'll be back quicker than a whisker cat can say fish."

"Not magic, Loekor, greed," she shook her head in disgust.
"If not magic, a weapon?" he asked.
"No."

"But surely, a rock like that has no value," he stated.

Cassis explained the value some races placed on the yellow metal.

"It is hard to believe," Loekor said, astonished a second time. "Are not friends, a dwelling place, food, and clean water more important?"

"Yes, Loekor, to some, to others no."

"This is strange," Loekor pondered over this new information, cautioning himself not to forget.

The gnome reappeared, slapping the dust from his green breeches and coat. "Now," he said, dragging up a chair and sitting across from Loekor and Cassis, "I suppose you want me to ferry you across the river." He reached up, stroking his beard, his eyes narrowing. "Of course, it will cost you another chunk of that precious metal, heh." He sat back, calculating.

"We know of no river," answered Loekor, perplexed. "What river is this you speak of?"

"Why, the river Udalay, of course." A worried frown crossed his face. He felt the gold slipping through his blunt fingers. "That is why you're here, is it not?"

"We were not aware that there was a river to cross," replied Cassis.

"In what direction do you travel?" the gnome asked, hoping it was in the right direction, his direction.

"West," answered Cassis and Loekor in unison.

"Well then of course there's a river to cross." His face fairly beamed. "It lies just over that furthest rise," he pointed over his shoulder for emphasis. "A dangerous river." He licked his lips, the greed shining like a beacon in his blue eyes. "The goblins found--," he did not fail to notice the way Loekor's hand tightened on the scepter when he mentioned goblins. He quickly recovered. "I don't mean to say they are friends of mine, but one has to make a living, heh."

"When?" Loekor asked.

"Let's see," he scratched his beard, his eyes turning up in contemplation. "I believe, let's see, yes I'm sure, the sun rose for a count of twenty-one." He was quick to notice the way his visitors relaxed. He continued, "As I was saying, there are many dangers to be found in the river. The only safe way to cross is on my ferry." He placed his arms on his knobby knees, rocking back and forth. "A living has to be made, heh."

"Yes," Cassis answered, not disguising the distaste in her voice.

"Good, good," the gnome said, crossing to a pantry, one with a lock. "Let us seal the bargain with some spirits, heh." Not waiting for an answer, he returned with a clay jug, setting this between them.

Loekor saw the mold decorating the outside of the jug and bit back the bile rising in his throat. The mold carried a great stench with it. "Later, mayhap," he struggled out.

Cassis just stared.

"Suit yourself." He upended the jug, noisily gulping the liquid. Wiping the small purple stream that had stained his beard with the dirty sleeve of his coat, he belched, setting the jug down. Rubbing his stubby hands together, he asked, "When do you wish to cross?"

Before they could answer, a heavy burden settled on the cabin's roof. The heavy timbers cracking with the weight. Loekor and Cassis looked at each other, then both looked toward the hole and just glimpsed the gnome's large feet vanishing.

The sound of something dragging, pulling itself along, assaulted their ears. Then the stench permeated the air, the waves of smell making the air almost unbreathable. Loekor clasped a hand over his mouth and nose, using the scepter as a crutch, he staggered toward the open doorway.

Cassis searched the passageways of her memory and then it came like a creeping black cloud, settling on her very being. "Get away from the opening," her voice quavered as she backed away to a far wall. Squatting down, she hurriedly scribbled runes on the floor, hoping this was enough protection.

Hearing the tone of her voice, Loekor could feel his heart thumping, the sound very loud in his ears. But even as he turned to comply, a loud hissing snaked through to his consciousness, his mind screaming at him to move in self-preservation.

Perhaps a second had passed since he had heard Cassis's warning, but to Loekor, it seemed like a lifetime, his body moving in slow motion. He felt, rather than saw, the long black arm with its rake of claws slicing toward his head. He heard Cassis scream and dropped to his knees, feeling his neck wrenched to one side, the muscles and tendons stretched, complaining.

He fell on his hands, shaking his head to clear it, and glimpsed a set of antlers lying on the floor. "Whose are those?" his fogged brain asked himself.

"Come on," Cassis grabbed Loekor by the arm, her voice pleading. "Hurry, or you will see no tomorrow."

Loekor let his instincts take over, crawling and dragging, with Cassis pulling until they were sitting against the wall furthest from the opening.

"The scepter, Loekor, use the scepter."

Loekor's dulled brain tried to comprehend this. His roving eyes finally laid to rest on the scepter gripped in his right hand, the orb pulsing red, signaling great danger. Staring at the orb entranced, realization dawned on Loekor, his drifting mind coming back to rest on their present danger. Standing, he held the scepter aloft, the orb now glowing white, brilliantly lighting the inside of the cabin.

The gnome raised his head above the level of the hold, his eyes wide in fright. The red hair adorning his head blazed in the scepter's light.

"No, no," he screamed. "If it be what I think, it will absorb the power." He scrambled out of the hold, dragging an earthen jar behind him, sloshing its contents on the floor.

The demon stuck its head into the doorway, its black lips drawn back, exposing its overly large canine teeth. Hissing, it spied its prey, as it began feasting on the scepter's power. Yellow slobber from its jaws rained down on the floor, pockmarking it with small blackened craters, as it tried to squirm through the door to reach its intended victims.

"Here, take this," said the gnome, giving the earthen jar to Loekor. "And throw its contents on the demon." By this time, the gnome was jumping from foot to foot. "Be quick before it's inside."

Loekor hefted the jug and then threw it, rewarded with seeing it break over the demon's head, drenching it in the sweet-smelling oil underlying the demon's breath.

Enraged, the demon hissed and renewed its efforts to get inside, the timbers lining the doorway creaking, shuddering, and finally splintering.

Smelling the oil, Loekor knew what he had to do. In two strides, he reached the lamp after narrowly ducking under the demon's claws and hurled it at the debauched creature.

   The oil caught and ignited, the flames fingering the sky as the demon staggered back, screeching in torment, its claws slicing the air. Spreading its wings, it vaulted into the air, looking like a fallen comet trailing its fiery tail as the demon plunged into the river beyond.

   "Born out of water, returned by fire," the gnome muttered, watching the demon's downward plunge.

   "How did you know the way to dispatch the demon?" Cassis asked, standing beside the gnome, with Loekor standing behind them.

   The gnome turned, regarding them. "There is nothing that comes from the water I do not know about."

   "We are fortunate that this is so," Loekor said, reaching up and feeling the small nubs, all that was left of his antlers. He knew he would sorely miss the antlers, but he also knew they would grow back in time, and he took heart in this knowledge.

   The gnome returned to the inside of the cabin, retrieving the jug of wine and turning it up noisily, relieved it of its contents, not spilling a drop. Finished, he turned to Cassis. "You have placed my pitiful life in jeopardy, witch." His now bloodshot eyes narrowed. "The black wizard will know."

   Cassis saw her chance at getting some information she was sure they could use. "Mayhap what you say is true, so it would be to your benefit to tell us what you know of the Dark One, what you call the black wizard."

   She patiently waited.

   Staggering to the table, the gnome braced himself on it. "Perhaps this is so," he slurred, the potency of the aged wine clearly evident. "I can only be dead once." He related all he knew of the Dark One, of the comings and goings, and most importantly, where the Dark One might be found. Finishing his tale, he asked, "and what good will this information do you?"

   Cassis, who had been standing straightened her shoulders, her voice taking on a tone of importance. "As I have said before, I am Cassis, Witch of the Blue Forest," she pointed to Loekor, "and he is Loekor of the Horned Ones," she paused for effect, "retainer of the Scepter of Soren."

   "So," said the gnome, not the least bit impressed.

   Cassis gritted her teeth until her jaws ached and just managed to hold her temper. "We are here, on our way to do battle with what you call the black wizard."

"So, let me see. You and the dehorned one over there are here to battle the black wizard, and yet you are not even able to destroy one demon." The gnome was quite drunk by now.

"It would be wise for you to help us if you can," Cassis fought her anger for control. "We must reach him before he can grow powerful again."

"It seems to me he is powerful now." The gnome released his hold on the table to stand on wobbly legs. He slurred out, "I will ferry you across the river on the morrow, and it will still cost you another piece of gold." The gnome found a corner in the room, which was no small feat for his condition, and falling down, he was soon snoring.

CHAPTER TWENTY-FIVE
The Ferryman

Loekor woke up, stretching his sore muscles, with his neck and shoulders being the sorest of all. He dispelled the doubts of the nightmare they had faced and defeated the night before. As he rose, he went to Cassis, who was standing in the doorway watching the day beginning. The dawn's brightness was overshadowed by low slung clouds, and a fine mist was falling from them. Together, they stood in silence, wrapped in their own thoughts.

Their meditation was interrupted by a loud curse, shattering the stillness and their thoughts. "So," the gnome hawked, clearing his throat and spitting on the floor, "we are still alive." Holding his head between stubby hands, he moaned, "The way I feel, it would be better if I were dead."

Resealing the trapdoor, the gnome barely gave Loekor time to grab his pack as he started to the river, with Loekor and Cassis trailing behind, wincing at the gnome's crude vocabulary. Ascending the last rise, the trio looked down from their small hillock to the river, its passing slow and sluggish, its color like that of new churned butter.

Pushing their way through the tall saw-toothed grasses, they stumbled down the overgrown path, with the grass whipping and slashing at their faces, blocking their access to the beach beyond. The gnome hurried to the ferry, his hands lovingly caressing the beams, lashed together with the same grasses lining the shore. Raising a tripod centered on the flat of the craft, he heaved a large rope, also made of woven grass, and treaded it into a large wooden pulley. On short legs, he hurried inland, raising a second tripod, and lashed it to stakes driven deep into the sandy soil. Checking the block and tackle and finding all satisfactory, he returned to the ferry, which resembled a ponderous raft.

Grasping a rope snaking up from the river, he pulled, his face turning bright red and sweating with the effort. The river grudgingly gave up the rope, parting the water with a dull twang as crustaceans of various sizes relinquished their grip, splashing back into the water. The smallest was the size of a pen, and the largest was easily as large as a dog. Loekor noted the formidable claws found on these creatures, happy he had another way of crossing besides swimming. Feeling the craft bump the shore, he let out a sigh as he gratefully stepped upon the bank, with Cassis following.

Cassis reached inside her robe, producing another piece of gold. The gnome, seeing this, raised a placating hand. "Keep your gold, witch. I will probably never live long enough to spend it." Cassis stared at the gnome dumbfounded. "If, that is, if you return, ring the bell found on yonder tree, and I shall return to fetch you back across." He gripped the rope, pulling, and then stopped. "Luck be with you, and save the gold witch." He grinned, showing even yellow teeth. "I shall require payment to ferry you back across."

They watched him cross, the wind carrying a mumbled curse now and then.

CHAPTER TWENTY-SIX
Hope and Courage

Turning away from the river, they made their way to the top of the opposite rise which they had left. Stepping down, Loekor felt as though he were stepping through a curtain. A curtain of impending doom and despair, a curtain of cold sorrows. His eyes traveled over the disheartening landscape, seeing huge blackened boulders scattered haphazardly as if tossed there by an unforgiving colossus. The stunted trees adorning the land dipped their branches as if in shame of the blight visited upon them.

"A sad place," Loekor thought, clutching the scepter, trying to draw strength from its power. As the day waned, the sky darkened, weeping. The luminous drops of rain tried in vain to add color and life to this desolate place. The robe Loekor wore grew heavy, cumbersome, mud covering its once-bright hem, the hem snagging bits of roots and sharpened rocks as he and Cassis stumbled through the quagmire of mud and long-dead grasses.

Relinquishing himself to the climate, he removed the robe, draping it over his broad shoulder. As he walked, he felt a tingling in his arm and, looking down, his eyes bulged in terror. The raindrops striking his exposed skin left small rivulets of red, tracing their way down his arm to drop from his fingertips. Even as he watched with horrid fascination, the skin on his arm cracked, splitting open, the exposed flesh quivering, turning to mush, and dropping in globs to plop on the ground.

"Cassis," he croaked, dropping to his knees. Cassis could see the stark terror in his eyes, the way his eyes wildly roved his body. He glanced at Cassis, his eyes pleading. "It is an illusion, Loekor," she screamed through the pelting rain, "nothing more." She surmised the spell, ripping the robe from Loekor's shoulder, and with this, she covered his convulsing body.

Her voice cut through his anxiety, and willing himself, he reduced the shaking to a tremble. Loekor looked at himself and felt the terror within him turn into hate, pointed at the evil found here. Laughter was discernible, mingling with the rain. Loekor felt the anger growing, encompassing him. His emotions exploded like a long-dead volcano as he threw back his head howling into the sky, challenging.

The sky paid no heed as the rain continued its steady barrage. Cassis helped him stand. "We must find shelter soon." She looked up into the anguished face, sympathy in her eyes, her thoughts cursing the Dark One. "Can you walk?" "Yes. I can walk." Grim determination set his face in stone. They trudged on, their footsteps making a sucking sound in the muck. Cassis cursed the rain, her limbs feeling leaden, each step draining her. "If only I could change," she thought, and then admonished herself for this, knowing the rain would not let her rise. Maybe that was for the best; the power of transformation should be saved.

Loekor took note of Cassis's haggard appearance and, bending down gently, lifted her, placing her on a wide shoulder, and continued on, surprised Cassis had not voiced an objection. "There," Loekor pointed at the small stand of trees. The ground was damp underneath, but the rain itself held at bay by the trees' fig-like leaves. Gratefully, he sunk down on the ground, helping Cassis from his shoulder as the rain beat a steady rhythm on the leaves overhead. Opening his pack, Loekor brought forth dried fruit, and this they ate while contemplating the dismal weather surrounding them.

Darkness fell like a plummeting falcon, and as if on cue, the rain ceased its steady drizzle. The only drops that now fell came from the fleshy leaves as they curled into slumber, their day's work done.

Loekor reached again for the hundredth time, feeling the nubs that had once supported his magnificent antlers. The quiet night intensified his loss as a feeling of deep sorrow descended on him with the absolute darkness. He shivered as he thought of the hopelessness of their quest. Shunning these thoughts aside, he let the spark of righteous anger in him take hold, igniting till it blazed within himself, burning away all else except his desire to confront the Dark One. He looked toward his companion, seeing only a very dim outline and hearing her soft breathing. He knew she was on her guard, sensing this; he too turned his own hearing to the outside noises.

As they watched the night, two bright green orbs appeared not far from them. Loekor, seeing these, tensed, slowing his breathing as he stared at the twin apparitions as they hovered and then moved. Loekor judged their size to be not much larger than his closed fist. He jumped as he felt a gentle touch on his arm and, following its movement, backed further into the trees while trying to quiet his hammering heartbeat.

The floating orbs were soon joined by hundreds of others. Loekor could feel the hair on the back of his neck stand on end as he saw in the cold green light what supported the shining eyes. A slight twittering reached his ears, and he saw the spider-like creatures disperse and then form a straight line as they slowly advanced toward them.

As the creatures came closer, Loekor found he could not tear his eyes away as he took in the ghastly skull-like heads, their whiteness made more apparent by the green faceted eyes that glowed from within the heads. An involuntary shudder shook him, seeing the human-shaped torso mated to the black, eight-legged horror beneath, the eight legs whispering across the damp ground.

So intense was his fascination coupled with revulsion, he did not notice the figure that had flanked them, even now drawing back its arm to hurdle the double-edged spear. Loekor felt a rush of air by his cheek and then heard the dull thud as the spear buried itself inches from his head.

Uttering his surprise, he reflexively reached out, grabbing Cassis's hand, and bounded from the trees in leaping strides, not knowing his direction but knowing that staying meant certain death, as he ran headlong through the night, with Cassis bumping at his side.

Slowing to catch his breath, he instinctively reached up, brushing his face where the spear point had furrowed its course, and it was then he noticed his case. His face was growing numb as well as his legs, the feeling spreading quickly throughout his body. Only by his effort of will did he continue, his breath now labored, rasping from his mouth.

Loekor and Cassis scrambled up the steep hillside, their hands clawing at the loose clusters of rocks that tumbled underfoot. The stones seemed to shift and slide with each step, threatening to send them tumbling back down to the valley below. At last, they reached the crest of the hill, where a pile of haphazardly stacked boulders offered a meager shelter. Slumping down behind the ring of boulders, Loekor felt his strength quickly ebbing away. He feebly reached for Cassis, his voice a hoarse whisper, "Cassis, the spear, it was poisoned."

In the gray light of dawn, Cassis examined the ragged gash, cursing herself for not having the herbs to cure Loekor, to battle the poison that now raced through his system. She wailed at her own inability as her mind raced with ideas, and then it came. One chance, she thought, prying the scepter from Loekor's stiffening fingers. "Let it work," she mumbled, placing the orb on Loekor's cheek even as his eyelids fluttered shut. Cassis looked with anguish at his chest, barely perceiving movement.

With all of Cassis's attention focused on Loekor, she failed to notice the eight-legged horrors surrounding the small boulder-strewn hillock, silently waiting for the command to rush the top. They had not long to wait as the air shimmered, soon replaced by a stench-filled cloud. The swirling mass rested inches off the ground, the ground below blackened, drained of any life that may have been found there.

"You have lost, Cassis," the voice screamed from the center of the miniature tornado. "Soon, the scepter shall be mine."

Cassis huddled over Loekor, tensed, biting back the hot retort that threatened to spew forth. Time, she thought, I need time to think. She raised herself until she was peeking over one of the boulders ringing their position. "Do you need these insects to do your work for you, foul one? Why not come and get the scepter yourself? Mayhap it be you fear one small witch." As she watched, the cloud darkened visibly.

"You will pay, Cassis, Witch of the Blue Forest," the Dark One snarled.

She hunkered back down, absently stroking Loekor's head. "I am sorry, Loekor," she mumbled, hot tears mingling with the dirt on her wizened face. "We were so close."

"Cassis," the voice was so weak it was barely discernible. Loekor drew in another tortured breath. "Let us not give up now," he said through clenched teeth.

As if on cue, the clouds parted, and the sun fought for dominance of the sky. The sun's beams stabbed at the damp ground while also reflecting off the tiny silver darts arcing towards the eight-legged shapes still waiting for the command to rush the top of the small hill. Even as the command was received, the arrows fell among the spider creatures, impaling a good many with their wicked barbs, throwing the others into confusion. As they scurried back and forth, their spears raised, but finding no enemies to hurtle them at.

"Bring me the scepter now," the Dark One roared, the small tornado ripping up tufts of grass and small clods of earth.

The spider creatures milled about, hesitant, staring at their fallen comrades. The small tornado spun faster, the rocks it now picked up hurled in all directions, some striking the creatures, knocking them senseless. "I said now," the tornado shrieked.

The inhuman army slowly advanced up the hill with raised spears. When they were a scant few feet from the top, a second hail of arrows poured down from the sky, the arrows seeking and finding their fleshy targets. The creatures closest to the top were impaled, the arrows so many it resembled long hair sprouting from their hideous bodies. Their death shrieks deafening as they rolled over onto their backs, their eight legs trembling and then curling back onto their hairy abdomens.

Cassis raised herself over the rim of a boulder upon hearing the commotion, and joy shone on her face when she saw their rescuers hurling themselves at the spider creatures with upraised swords. Through the din of battle, she spied King Illson astride his mount, the norn busily shaking loose an eight-legged creature stuck on his horn, giving it a taste of another kind of poison while his master hacked and hewed at the creatures unfortunate enough to be caught within the spinning silver arc of death his hand wielded.

"Cassis—Cassis," Loekor rasped.

"We are safe now, Loekor. King Illson has come with an army. An army of all," she said, squatting down with her tear-stained face close to Loekor. "Hang on, Loekor." She placed a hand on his sweaty forehead. "You must."

Therseus was the first to reach the top, the joy on his face quickly fading as he took in Loekor's inert form with Cassis huddled over him. Jumping over the boulders, he knelt by Loekor's side, grasping his friend's limp hand. "Loekor."

Hearing Therseus' voice, Loekor slowly opened his bloodshot eyes. "Therseus, my young friend." He took a shuddering breath and smiled. "I thought you had perished." His eyes slowly closed once more.

"No, my friend, I did not perish, and neither will you." He reached over, pulling Cassis to him, embracing her.

They heard a scurrying and were soon joined by Maloc. "It is good to see you, my friends." Rustling through his robes, he produced a small wooden bowl, to which he added a white powder and dissolved it with wine. He pressed this into Cassis' hand. "Get him to drink this."

Cassis took the bowl, looking at it not comprehending. "It is a cure for the poison that ails him."

They watched quietly as Cassis raised Loekor's head, tilting the wooden bowl to his lips. "Drink, Loekor," she whispered to him, "Drink."

A litter was brought to the top, and the solemn procession made its way down.

Voices talking quietly woke Loekor from his healing sleep. Though it agonized him greatly, he turned his head and saw Therseus slumped over, asleep by his side. "Therseus," his hoarse voice rasped out. "Is it you?"

Startled awake, Therseus jumped, then looked down at his friend, a smile creasing his boyish face. "You're back." He reached out gently, laying a hand on Loekor's shoulder. "We've been worried, but I knew no poison would take you."

At the slight commotion, they were joined by others. Cassis squatted down, taking Loekor's hand. "How do you feel?"

"Hungry," Loekor replied. His answer brought chuckles from those assembled around him. Looking up into the faces, he saw King Illson with Maloc by his side and standing next to him the dark-haired giant from Therseus' village, as well as the gnome, which surprised him greatly.

Soon, a steaming bowl of broth was pushed into Cassis' hands, and she fed it to Loekor until he had his fill. "I thank you, all of you," he said before drowsiness overtook him.

The days chased by like a long-tailed cat trying to catch the elusive tail following him before Loekor again awakened, this time finding himself refreshed and eager for what lay ahead. He rose, stretching cramped limbs, a smile on his face, happy to be out of the dark pit the poison had thrust him into.

He stared at his surroundings, confounded at finding himself in a large tent, the floor carpeted, while braziers of fire burned in its four corners, warming the tent. Voices outside intruded upon the quiet he was relishing, and then he remembered.

"Let it not be a dream," he thought, crossing the floor and pushing the tent flaps aside, the sun's bright glare temporarily blinding him, the voices now quieted. A moment of panic seized him before his eyes adjusted to the outside light, the shadows before him now coming into focus.

The first to cross the short distance and reach him was Therseus. He stopped a few feet from Loekor, measuring him. It was then that Loekor realized how close a friendship it was that bonded them. "I am well," Loekor choked out, reaching out and laying his hands on Therseus's broad shoulders.

Therseus could not restrain the emotions inside himself as a joyous cry escaped his lips while embracing his friend. "I am happy to see you well, my friend," he said through a tear-choked voice.

"And I you, young Therseus," his own voice wavering with emotion.

Later that day, stories were recounted to Loekor of the dreams and visions that had prompted the mixed army beings to gather and seek out Loekor and Cassis. Of Soren coming to each of them warning of the dire plight Loekor and Cassis would be thrust into.

Loekor thanked each of them, starting with the reptilian Kazoon and ending with the gnome. King Illson told of the battle with the spider creatures and how they had let the survivors scurry back to their holes.

Loekor was happy to hear there were no losses of life on King Illson's side. Their strategy and element of surprise were so complete. "How was it the Dark One was caught unaware?" asked Loekor.

"It was Maloc," answered Lark. "He blocked him from seeing."

"I wish I could take this credit, but it was Soren who told me how I might accomplish this. It was also he who told me what healing powders to bring," intoned Maloc.

Loekor approached Maloc, laying a large hand on Maloc's shoulder, the hand dwarfing Maloc's small frame. "Still, I thank you for my life. It took great courage to go against the Dark One." Bowing to all those gathered, he continued, "All of you have shown courage and bravery that will not soon be forgotten." He placed himself in the center of all those gathered. "Soren also came to me in a dream." The murmurs grew silent.

"My quest is almost over. It is now my battle to fight, and fight I will. I will risk no life but my own." There was a loud protest from all those there. Loekor raised a hand, quieting them. "This is how it must be." He looked at Cassis. "You have brought me far, Cassis, but now it is up to me."

She nodded her agreement.

He then turned his gaze toward Therseus and bit back the smile at seeing the girl elf gripping his hand tightly. "We have shared many adventures, and it is my hope we will share many more." His voice grew hoarse. "I count you as a friend and warrior." Therseus stepped forward, embracing Loekor. There was general agreement that they would wait here for his return.

The next morning, as dawn streaked the sky with its gray pallor, the lone wizard started the final leg of his quest, the many-colored robe bringing a brightness to the dreary landscape. The inner light of the orb, mounted on the scepter, was subdued as if it knew it must reserve its energy for the battle that was to come.

Therseus and Theena watched Loekor until he disappeared into the landscape. "Good luck, my friend," he murmured before they turned, trudging back to the camp.

CHAPTER TWENTY-SEVEN
The Fall of the Dark One

Loekor let his instincts guide him as his eyes studied the dead landscape. The trees were blackened and leafless, their skinny limbs bowing to the gray earth. A fog wrapped the land in a continual blanket, making it hard to see but a few feet in any direction. Loekor would have tripped several times over tree roots seeking nourishment from the air itself, if not for the orb adorning the scepter that dimly lit his way.

"It is a sad place," he thought to himself while navigating his way over a muddied stream, its water as if it had the texture of molasses. The closer he got to his destination, the feeling of being watched grew more pronounced. He missed the company of Cassis and Therseus as he trudged on, the ground softening and squelching with every step. He hummed a tune, trying to keep his anxiety under control.

"Easier to stop a volcano from erupting," he thought to himself, aware of his humming echoing back to him from the nightmarish landscape, the swirling mist playing tug of war with his legs. "I will not turn back," he resolved to himself, even though his instincts were screaming at him to turn and race back to safety.

"Your powers dwindle, Dark One," he said aloud and flinched as it boomed back at him. He felt better even though it was his own voice that shattered the eerie silence. "If it had been possible to store all the gloom in the world in one place, then this would be it," thought Loekor as he stared up at the dark mountainside. His keen sight barely perceiving the opening of a cave several hundred feet up the slope, the entrance trickling a small light into the darkness.

Steeling himself for what might come, he took the first tentative step upwards. "I could show you the difference between hooves and feet now, Therseus," chuckled Loekor, the hollow sound reassuring as he dug another hoof into the loose soil, the going slow and treacherous.

Stopping, he looked upwards, the cave mouth easily seen now, the flickering light guiding his way like a beacon. A short time later, he found himself standing on the ledge just outside the entrance, his breathing slow but labored as he pressed himself against the wall just outside the entrance. Straining his hearing, he could hear no sounds save for a bubbling coming from the interior. His sense of smell was attacked by a fetid odor coming in waves. Swallowing his gorge, he leaned over peering into the cave's dank interior.

"Welcome, Loekor of the Horned Ones," said a soft voice from within. "Please, I bid you enter."

With his courage wrestling the fear inside him, Loekor took a deep breath of the stench-filled air and stepped into the mouth of the cave. Three things he noticed at once: the grizzly throne and the black-clad figure sitting upon it, a cowl covering his head, and the foul-smelling bird creature perched on an outcropping of rock, staring at him through slitted eyes.

"Let us not be formal," said the dark-clad figure, reaching up with long, tapered fingers and removing the cowl.

Loekor was prepared for anything except the boyish face that now regarded him with ice-blue eyes and a pleasant smile, the kind that stretched from ear to ear, revealing a perfect set of pearly white teeth. The smile was genuine, exuding warmth and kindness, yet Loekor couldn't shake the feeling that something was off. The Dark One's eyes traveled from Loekor to the scepter, drinking in its power.

Noticing this, Loekor gripped the scepter even harder, his knuckles cracking noisily in the small confines. Nonchalantly, the Dark One reached up, brushing a lock of golden hair from his wide, flat forehead. Crossing his long legs, he asked, "So, where is it we go from here?"

"You go back from whence you came," answered Loekor, admiring the flawless lines of the youthful face.

"That may not be as easy a task as what you might think." He rose from the throne, not taking his eyes from Loekor.

Loekor measured the Dark One, finding him almost as tall as himself. "No one said it would be easy." He felt the fear returning but masked it in an easy pose, a smile on his face.

"Mayhap it be you have come here to die," shrieked the Dark One, catching Loekor by surprise. Throwing his cape back, he extended his arms, flexing the long, tapered fingers in a blur of motion, blue sparks dancing between them. "Die!" he screamed, sending the blue line of fire arcing towards the scepter's glowing orb.

Loekor stumbled back, the fingers gripping the scepter encased in blue flame, the pain unbearable. With a scream erupting from his twisted mouth, he saw out of the corner of his eye a movement, and drawing upon his willpower, he swung the scepter, catching the harpy full in the face, knocking it out of the cave, across the ledge, and down the slope in a squawking ball of feathers.

Through sheer willpower, he returned his attention to the Dark One, summoning the scepter's power, sending the blue flame back to its source, bringing the Dark One to his knees.

"You are more powerful than I thought," the Dark One spewed out, his fetid breath sickening Loekor to his very being.

"Give it up, foul one," Loekor said through clenched teeth, the pain in his hand slowly abating.

"A thousand years I have waited for you to free the scepter," he stood on wobbly legs. "It shall be a fitting trophy."

"Take it then," Loekor screamed. Raising the scepter, he brought forth its power in a glowing ball, the blue sphere dancing with the lightning bolts held in its center. This he hurled at the Dark One, using the scepter as one would a bat, the ball hitting the Dark One squarely in the chest, splintering it and releasing the energy.

The Dark One screamed, flailing at the tiny bursts of energy attacking like a swarm of angry bees. He stopped swinging at the energy bolts and glared at Loekor through hate-filled eyes, the eyes slowly turning from blue to a flowing red. "You will pay," his hoarse voice whispered, removing his cape and throwing it on the floor, reciting an incantation.

As Loekor watched, a swirling vortex appeared over the cape, the stench-filled cloud growing in size. Sensing movement from the floor, he watched in horror as the cape shifted, changed, also growing in size. He backed from the cave until he was standing on the ledge, just outside.

The vortex continued to grow, burrowing its way through the roof of the cave. As Loekor watched, the mountain top exploded in a hail of rocks and dirt. The vortex continued to grow, sucking something monstrous from the cave until it was perched on top, the long talons gripping the rim of the newly formed crater while unfolding its scaled wings.

"Now you will see my power, pitiful creature," the Dark One said. Loekor followed the voice, his blood turning cold at the sight of his adversary perched on top of the huge dragon.

The vortex spun away, leaving the air still and quiet except for the sound of the dragon's large wings raking the air. The dragon roared, shaking the very mountain, then looked down, seeing Loekor, its mouth slavering, its unblinking orange eyes fastening onto him. Drawing in an impossible amount of air, the dragon doubled its size and then released a sheet of flame, scarring the mountainside but leaving Loekor untouched.

"The robe," he thought, bringing his arm down and uncovering his head. "The robe saved me." With shaking hands, he raised the scepter. "Soren, I call on you."

Nothing happened.

The dragon launched itself from the rim, its wings beating heavily at the air. Resigning himself to the death that now circled above him, he felt a hot anger rise and take hold, giving him strength. He screamed, releasing the pent-up anger, and threw the scepter as one would a spear, at the soft underbelly of the dragon.

The dragon dodged the scepter easily, banking to the far right, intent upon plucking his quarry from the small ledge. Instead of falling, the scepter continued its upward course, disappearing into the night and already forgotten by Loekor, who was looking for something to battle the dragon and its rider with. His hands closed on two large rocks, and these he clenched tightly in his fists as he watched the dark shape hurtling at him, its talons flexed and ready to grasp. "I will not die so easily," he whispered to himself. He wasn't sure, but thought he heard a cackling from the dragon's back.

The dragon was only a second from snatching him when he

launched his missiles, and at almost the same instant, heard a whistling by his ear and saw the dragon falter, an arrow buried in its belly, while its rider was almost unseated as one of the two rocks found their mark. This gave him the chance he needed to duck the steel-like talons, though the wind generated by the wings almost blew him from the ledge. While keeping an eye on the wounded dragon, he chanced a glance over the ledge and spotted Therseus scrabbling up the side of the mountain, a bow in his hand.

He also spied Cassis in close pursuit. At almost the same time, he saw the dragon banking again, the dark silhouette on its back pointing toward Therseus and Cassis. "Go back," he shouted, "go back," but Therseus and Cassis were heedless of this warning, wanting to help their friend.

Only seconds had passed while all this transpired, but for Loekor, it seemed like eternity.

The scepter forgotten still traveled its upward spiral, almost checked. As it reached the apex of its flight, it hung in the air, much as a cloud would. The orb pulsed, radiating a blinding light, dispelling the blackness, and through this light, a roar sounded. A roar that would have sent a grackette scurrying.

Loekor looked up with disbelief, seeing the shadow coming through the brilliant light take shape and form. The gryphon streaked down with folded wings, cutting the air like a rocket on its downward plunge.

The dragon turned from its intended quarry, its attention now focused on this new enemy, tasting the air with his long, black forked tongue. Therseus and Cassis reached the ledge and stood with Loekor in open-mouthed wonder at the new titan, seeming born of the very sky itself. Straining their eyes, they could see the dark silhouette perched on the dragon's back, striking its neck, his blows ineffectual as the dragon roared its acceptance of the challenge.

Beating his wings furiously, he ascended in a blur of motion to meet the new adversary, his now unwilling rider drawn into this aerial battle of giants.

The very air itself seemed to scream in agony as the two hurled themselves at each other, both their wings now slicing through the air. Just when it seemed they would collide, the gryphon used his catlike reflexes, banking to the left, evading the dragon's extended talons while raking his claws down the dragon's side, leaving deep, bloody furrows in the armor-like hide, drenching the three spectators below in a rain of blue-black blood.

The dragon, wounded and enraged, bellowed in pain and anger, hovering in the sky, searching for the gryphon, but not seeing the golden blur that even now streaked toward its unprotected back from above, its claws extended to their fullest.

The gryphon did not go unnoticed by the Dark One as he screamed and pleaded with the dragon, but his pleas went unheeded as a gnat to a bull that has been provoked. His eyes grew impossibly wide, his voice choked with terror as the golden missile closed the distance to within a second of impact.

In less than the blink of an eye, right before imminent collision, the gryphon unfurled its full sixty-foot wingspan, slowing the large body and enabling it to sink its four sets of claws deeply into the scaled hide of the dragon, while sending its rider cartwheeling and screaming to the ground far below. The dragon, with the added burden on the gryphon's weight, flailed the air in a useless effort to stay aloft as it followed its rider's path to the depths below, the gryphon's beak deeply embedded in its neck even as its scales were ripped from its body in bloody tatters by the gryphon claws.

Loekor, Cassis, and Therseus stood as mute witnesses to this display of ferocity on the gryphon's part as they watched the Dark One, followed by the plummeting titans, strike the ground. The small earthquake caused by this dislodging a portion of the ledge almost toppled them had they not had fast reflexes, jumping back in time.

They stood quiet, each wrapped in their own thoughts for several minutes before Loekor reached down, plucking Cassis from the ledge and wrapping his other arm around Therseus' quaking shoulders.

Finally, Loekor broke the silence. "Let us climb down."

"But Loekor —," started Therseus before he was interrupted.

"Do not fear the gryphon," answered Loekor, nudging him down the mountain, Cassis still carried in his other arm, quiet. "He is — or mayhap was — a friend."

The dust had barely settled as these three made their way to where the giants had collided with the earth. Timidly they moved closer and were surprised to see only one giant shape, its body twisted and broken, not moving. Their eyes traveled as one before stopping on the gryphon, who was in the process of delicately licking the blue-black blood of the dragon from its tawny coat while regarding them with thoughtful eyes.

"It is good to see you again, Loekor, and you Cassis," said a disembodied voice.

"He talks," said Therseus, stepping a little behind Loekor while reaching for and finding Cassis' hand which he squeezed tightly.

"Come, Loekor, help me down," said a now muffled voice. Loekor placed Cassis on the ground. Approaching the winged lion by himself and reaching up, he stroked the lion affectionately. "Thank you, Auk."

Auk chirped, lowering its large head, gently nuzzling Loekor. Reaching up into the glossy black mane, he gently wrapped his hands around the shimmering robe, a robe such as his own, and helped Soren down. Before Loekor could speak, Soren smiled, producing the scepter.

"I believe this is yours."

Therseus and Cassis still stood in numbed silence. Soren looked over at the two companions and beckoned them closer. "Cassis, has it been so long that you have forgotten old friends and comrades? And you, young Therseus, come so that we might talk."

"Soren," Cassis mumbled, taking a slow step forward and then hurrying over to Soren, embracing him and leaving Therseus standing where he was, his eyes still wide, his voice still lost.

Seeing this, Loekor walked over, taking Therseus' arm. "Come, Therseus, meet our friend," he half walked, half dragged the young man over to Soren and the gryphon.

Soon they were all friends, relating the adventures that had befallen them, almost forgetting the Dark One until Therseus asked what had happened to him.

There was a twinkle in Soren's eyes, and instead of answering, he walked over to Auk. "Auk, raise your paw." The gryphon complied, releasing a small black beetle that had been imprisoned by the large pad, the beetle's eyes glowing a bright red.

Made in the USA
Coppell, TX
17 May 2023